# Janet Hall

a novel

## Chella Courington

Janet Hall
Copyright © 2024 by Chella Courington



This is a work of fiction.  Any resemblance to actual persons, living or deceased, is purely coincidental.

ISBN: 979-8-9894513-6-4
Library of Congress Control Number: 2024942059

Published in 2024 by All Things That Matter Press.

# Acknowledgments

I want to thank the following dear ones for their influence and/or assistance: my readers whose suggestions and insights are found within this novel: David Borofka, Stephanie Alexich-Clark, Allison Hubbard, Claudia Hoag McGarry, Robin Tiffany, and Mary & Sam Waters; my publishers and editors, Deb and Phil Harris of *All Things That Matter Press*, especially Deb for her meticulous editing; and my writing mentors: Robin Lippincott, Alicia Ostriker, and Virginia Woolf.

Finally, I want to thank my partner, Ted Chiles, for his steadfast belief in my novel: reader, editor, mentor, and lover. Without you I could not have written *Janet Hall*.

Riches is nothing in the face of the Lord, for He can see into the heart.
—William Faulkner, *As I Lay Dying*

Poor people only have their family and human dignity. They can't even call the land their own.
—Jacob Hall, "The Land"

The mystery in how little we know of each other is no greater than the mystery of how much.
—Eudora Welty, *The Optimist's Daughter*

I didn't want to open my eyes. Throbbing temples, dry mouth, and weak limbs all spoke of tequila. The sheets were ironed and smelled of lavender, so I wasn't at home. But I wasn't going to open my eyes until some fragment of last night rose up and apprised me of my current circumstances.

"I can tell you're awake."

"Please don't yell."

"William, I told you not to play nine-ball for tequila shots," she said.

—Jacob Hall, "Behold, I Give You the Power"

# Chapter 1

Trion, Alabama
Saturday, September 7, 2019
12:30 a.m.

My name is Janet Grace Hall, with Hall being my married name. Although I've been divorced thirty-five years, I stayed a Hall instead of taking back my maiden name, Williams. I'm considered a feminist failure by my peers, but they obviously don't know the Williamses. Besides, I still love Jacob, my ex.

Born and raised in Trion, Alabama, I escaped and never imagined I'd live here again. Then, three years ago, Aunt Grace, my father's sister, passed away and bequeathed everything to me. A house is a gift hard to refuse, even if it's in Alabama, and that's why I moved back at sixty-one after retiring from teaching in Columbia, South Carolina. I'd planned to sell the house, but, over two years later, I'm still here.

An Appalachian town of twenty thousand, Trion lies northeast of Birmingham on Highway 431, atop Sand Mountain, which, worn flat and covered by fields, pastures, and Tyson chicken plants, doesn't resemble a mountain. If a breeze is up, you smell the birds. This night, like most nights, the lights shut off around eleven p.m. when the dogs are put out or let in, depending on the owner's age and attitude. Either yard dogs or furry family. In the past, folks left their doors unlocked, yet Trion has changed.

Older Trion homes are known more by family name than by address, and tonight the Williams house is dark except for the light at the front door. Inside, I lie in my aunt's four-poster spool bed with Rhoda, my gray tabby. A book is open on my chest and a hangover slowly blooms. I should get a couple of Tylenol, but Rhoda is next to me, and if I get up, she will desert the bed and leave me alone. These days, I take what warmth is offered.

The phone rings. Rhoda raises her head with distaste and settles back into the folds of the old patchwork quilt. I pick up my iPhone. "Hey, Jacob."

"How did you know it was me?"

"Caller ID. But who else calls me this fucking late?"

"Someone could have died," he says. This is true. We've entered that age when death becomes a more frequent visitor. Musicians and writers and actors are falling with greater commonness. Our friends will follow. Our parents are gone, and someday we will be gone, too.

"You still there?" Jacob asks.

"How much have you had to drink?"

"No more than usual."

"A lot then." I take the phone and go to the bathroom, swallow two Tylenol, and sit on the toilet.

"I worked through all your suggestions and think the story's done."

"Fine. Send it out," I say and cover the phone with my hand to hide the sounds.

"I want you to read it again."

I stand, close the lid, consider flushing, and don't.

"Why? I made five minor comments."

"Please. I've already emailed it to you."

I hear the pop and crack of a fire in the background. When we were in grad school, we used to make love, sweat dripping, in front of the fireplace.

"How cold is it there?" I ask.

"Down to fifty tonight."

"It's warm here. You wouldn't need a fire if you moved back to Trion, and you wouldn't have to phone me in the middle of the night. Just shake me awake."

His silence is palpable whenever I mention coming back home. Jacob has over thirty years at Illinois State and can retire whenever he chooses. He's a good teacher and could be a great one if he wanted. Nevertheless, writing comes first.

"Why don't you move here?" he asks. "Then you could please your brother and sell Aunt Grace's house."

"You know how much I like the feel of this house. Besides, it's too cold in Illinois."

"Yeah … it makes the spring … truly better," he says, lowering his voice with each word. His "poet" voice.

"We have family here: your sister and niece, my brother. We know people."

"I know people here," he says. "Anyway, I'm not close to my sister anymore. You're my family, Janet."

"And your twins."

"Not nearly as much as you," he says.

I don't answer. We've had this conversation before. I'm tired, and the Tylenol isn't working on my head, only souring my stomach.

"Why don't we move somewhere new like California?" he asks.

"Too expensive, plus we're too old to start completely over," I say. "Why not here?"

"I love you, but I can't. I can't go home again."

I've heard all this, time and again. His "failed" career includes literary prizes, a *New Yorker* story, and a collection of short stories all by the age of thirty with a fresh Ph.D.—enough to carry him through tenure. Then no more books. No short story collections. No novel. Just well-crafted stories that became less and less frequent as his early confidence—really arrogance—melted away like glaciers to global warming, and his dependence on me grew and grew.

"Nobody in Trion cares. You're still their golden boy," I say.

"Thomas Wolfe got it right. 'You can't go home again.'"

"I did."

"You're stronger than I am."

I'm exhausted. I love him, but he has to make some concessions. I'm his editor, his writing support, and his lover. I'm tired, too tired for this shit.

"Maybe we should take a break," I say.

"Is that a threat?"

"No, this is. Either come back to Trion or I'm done. Find someone else to hold your hand." I cut the phone off, mute it, and go to the kitchen for some saltines to calm my stomach.


The Williams House
Saturday, September 7, 2019
1:00 p.m.


At the kitchen table, I'm marking essays. Like many English teachers who retire, my profession has become my hobby. I don't play golf or tennis. I have no interest in baking bread or pastries. Except for snipping off deadheads and tossing wildflower seeds into the backyard, I'm not much of a gardener. I don't play bridge and haven't any inclination to learn. After several months of questioning whether I retired too early, I took an adjunct position teaching one section of composition every semester at Trion State Community College.

Interrupting my rhythm, the phone rings. The name Susan, Jacob's sister who's two years younger than I, appears on the screen, and I consider letting her call go to voicemail. She blames me for divorcing Jacob, for sleeping with him after the divorce, for ruining his second marriage, for being a Democrat, and probably for being friends with "Mexicans," what polite town folk of Trion call Latinx.

The ringing stops, then starts again. I hit the green button.

"Susan, how—"

"Jacob's dead."

"What?"

Susan's tears muffle her voice. She repeats, "Jacob's dead. The woman who cleans his house found him on the floor in his study, Willy next to him. They think it was a heart attack."

"I just talked to him last night."

"Did you upset him?"

"No." I lie. "He called about midnight."

"What did you talk about?"

"His writing. Everyday stuff."

"Jacob would've been perfectly happy here if you hadn't dragged him away," Susan says and disconnects.

I want to tell her that Aunt Grace encouraged me to get out of town as she did to see how the rest of the world lived. Then, if I wanted to come back, I always could.

Reaching down, I run my hand over Rhoda's back to feel her warm fur. Looking at the phone, I put it on the table, open the fridge, then shut it.

I call Jacob. Five rings before the phone goes to voicemail. "This is Jacob. You know the drill." I disconnect and call again. And again. Waiting for him to pick up.

A vague image, misty and dark, of a pool table and a neon Schlitz sign came to me. The mattress shifted, and I felt her lips on my ear. Her kiss raised goosebumps.

"I got you a Coke and a couple of aspirin, or do you need a Bud?"

Georgia? Georgia who tends bar at the County Line?

"Come on Professor. I got a place I need to be," Georgia said.

—Jacob Hall, "Behold, I Give You the Power"

# Chapter 2

Trion High School
Wednesday, April 14, 1971
10:00 a.m.

Like high schools everywhere, Trion High had a defined social order. First, there was class standing, seniors outranked juniors and juniors outranked sophomores. Freshmen were expected to keep their heads down and their mouths shut. Upward mobility was possible through sports, with football being most important and basketball second. For females, majorettes were the highest ranked followed by flagbearers then cheerleaders. It was a white male hierarchy. The athletes gave pride to the school while the pretty, peppy girls gave sexual appeal. Every other student was on a sliding scale beneath the upper echelon with the smart students either playing dumb to fit in or occupying a minor role in the system of secondary education—class officers and newspaper/yearbook editors.

Jacob Hall, a junior, was near the top of the heap. A defensive back on the varsity football team as a sophomore, Jacob was legendary for his ability to tackle and read the opponent's offense. As a junior, he became a co-captain. Jacob was also the editor of the school paper and the male lead in Trion High's production of *Oklahoma*. He was one of the golden boys.

I was a freshman fortunate to have a fiercely protective and popular older brother. Mike was a junior and a varsity defensive tackle. Beyond that connection, I had no status. I was pretty enough yet didn't work at it. Smart yet without outward demonstration in my classes. Answering questions when asked, I rarely sat in the front. My hand didn't shoot up and bring unwanted attention every time I knew the answer. According to social norms, I was an ideal freshman. A diligent student with a few diligent girlfriends, I'd hole up in the library or my room and read after schoolwork was finished. When Jacob approached me at my locker, I was shocked.

"Janet," Jacob said quietly, touching my shoulder.

I remember turning quickly, surprised to see him, my algebra and history books slipping out of my arms and crashing on the hardwood floor. Before I could pick them up, he handed them to me, squatting and rising with the grace of a giant cat. He was beautiful. Hair the shade of milk chocolate and eyes to match.

"Did I scare you?" he asked.

"No," I said. "You startled me."

I was unaccustomed to the attention of boys. Those my age were mostly children and the few who might take interest were afraid of Mike.

"Here I am." He smiled, the right side of his mouth tilting upward. "Would you go with me to a party Friday night?"

I couldn't believe what I heard. Go to a party with Jacob Hall? Maybe he was high, though he didn't have that kind of reputation.

"Will you?" he asked.

"I need to ask Mike."

"Why?"

"Because he's my big brother." Immediately I wanted to erase what I said, sounding like some elementary school kid. Whether Jacob thought my response immature or strange, he never showed it.

"We better get to class," he said. "I'll call tonight."

I watched his back as he turned the corner. Jacob Hall asked me, a lowly freshman, to a party. Mike, who called me a "nerdy bookworm," would be impressed that someone popular like Jacob would ask me anywhere. I was excited and scared. Why me? I thought maybe I knew. Big man on campus wanted more worshipers? He was going to be surprised then. Ultimately, we were both surprised.


Janet's House
Friday, April 16, 1971
6:00 p.m.


In a yellow and blue paisley dress with an empire waist, I stood in front of my mirror, hating the way I looked. Mother had applied makeup—base, rouge, brown eyeliner, green eyeshadow, and glossy pink lipstick—with strict instructions to wash my face before coming home in case Father waited up for me.

"I don't think he'd like you all made up," she said, powdering my nose.

I didn't like myself all made up—a girl painted to please a boy. If that's what Jacob wanted, then I was the wrong girl.

Fifteen minutes later, I heard him talking to her. Father was still absent, "playing cards with the boys" from the Goodyear Plant in Gadsden. Having changed to neatly pressed blue jeans and a white blouse with purple embroidery around the collar, all four of the buttons fastened and hiding a small silver chain with a peace sign, I felt more myself. The shirt was from Key West and the necklace from Greenwich Village—both gifts from Aunt Grace.

I started down the stairs, and Jacob looked up. At that moment I felt something new, something shift—tectonic plates meeting perhaps and transforming the landscape. Even so it would take years to understand how our attraction altered our being. There on those steps, many layers beneath my outward presence and barely available to the innocent girl, was the suspicion that my life would never be the same.

He was dressed in newish jeans, no visible fade, and a white Oxford shirt, sleeves rolled to his elbow. In his left hand was a bunch of wildflowers, the comics page from the *Trion Reporter* wrapped around the stems. As I came toward him, he looked pleased and surprised. I wasn't carrying a purse. Instead, I carried a copy of *The Optimist's Daughter*.

I smiled and thanked him, took the flowers to the kitchen, and put them in a blue Mason jar that I half-filled with water and placed on the dining table where Jacob could see them.

"Where's your purse?" Mother asked, her voice tinny as if she wanted to say more. I heard the hesitation, the suppressed desire to unleash her anger at me who dared to defy her mother. No dress, no makeup. Nevertheless, I knew that Jacob, Mike's friend with a bounty of charm, was enough to quell a southern lady raised on pleasing men. Unlike Father, Mother would punish me in small ways, burn my toast or over starch my clothes. He would send Jacob away and beat me. And probably beat her for failing in her duties.

"I have everything I need in my pockets," I said.

"I won't keep her out late, Mrs. Williams," Jacob said, pushing open the screen door.

Mother followed us out to the porch and watched as I got into Jacob's truck and we drove away. I turned and waved. She raised her hand in return. I knew she would stay on the porch until we were out of sight because she always did; yet there was a moment in panic that I turned again to see if her anger had driven her back into the house. She stood there, her hand lifted in the dusk's golden hue.

Jacob pulled in front of Ken Mosley's house. Seven trucks and cars, two of which were matching Crimson Tide red Caddies parked under a huge awning. Having seen them around town, I knew the Caddies belonged to Ken's parents. The house, one of the largest in Trion, covered most of two lots.

"Why aren't their cars in the garage?" I asked

"They converted it for the live-in help," Jacob said.

I felt more out of place at that moment than I'd ever felt—sitting next to a boy who should not have been seen talking to me in the hall, outside a house four times larger than the one I was raised in, and dressed in jeans like my Aunt Grace, the "commie" librarian of Trion who returned to the mountain to shed light in the wilderness.

"This is a first," Jacob said. "A date bringing a book. Do you expect to be bored?"

The corners of his mouth turned upward in an almost smile.

"It's for you. I finished it and thought you might like it. Eudora Welty's one of us." I had no idea where "one of us" came from. I meant Welty was from the South.

Jacob took the book and held it up to the dim illumination. "Thanks," he said. "I'll bring you one when I'm done."

"Why are we here, Jacob?"

"To go to a party."

"Why me? You could ask anyone, even a senior, and any of them would say yes."

"I wanted to ask you," Jacob said in his soft voice, his eyes as intent on me as mine on him.

"You're not getting to second base with me," I said, hoping I wasn't blushing.

Neither of us spoke. The cooling engine clicked and a cricket started up outside my window.

Jacob broke the silence. "I didn't want to bring anyone. I wanted someone I could talk to about what's important to me."

"And what's that?"

"Books. Writing."

"So you see me reading a book, and you ask me out."

"No. I keep seeing your name on all the library books I check out. *To Kill a Mockingbird, Franny and Zooey, Slaughterhouse-Five, The Heart Is a Lonely Hunter.*"

I imagined my face glowed then like a doll's with bright, pink cheeks. Not an entirely unfamiliar feeling. Throbbing with heat and garnering all the wrong kind of attention, I felt on red alert.

"We better get in there before Mike comes looking for us," Jacob said.

He jumped out of the truck and opened my door. I unfastened my top two buttons to reveal my necklace with the silver peace sign and stepped onto the pavement, never dropping my chin. We stood face to face, nearly touching.

As we climbed the steps to Ken's house, Jacob squeezed my hand before ringing the doorbell. I fought the urge to run back to his truck when Ken opened the door.

"You're late, buddy. And who do we have here?" Ken asked, filling the doorway like a bouncer at a college bar.

"Hi, Ken. Expecting someone else?" I asked.

"You going to let us in?" Jacob punched Ken on the shoulder.

"Welcome to the Moseley Mash." He stepped aside and winked at me, Jacob still holding my hand.

The Moseley family has made a living off the dead for three generations. Ken's grandfather built the original Moseley Funeral Home downtown on Main Street in 1934. Twenty years later, Ken's father relocated the business to Highway 431. Ken was the third Moseley to take charge. Taller than six feet with dirty blond hair, he had the charm and gentle authority that would contribute to his later success.

We followed him into the living room, where I stopped. Being my first time at Ken's, or at any house that size, I was struck by the difference between this room and the one in my house. The Moseley's room was arranged elegantly with antiques handed down from Ken's grandfather and glistening from polish. The rugs showed wear yet were neither threadbare nor ragged. Consumed by avarice, I wanted to stay there, sit on the velvet settee, and ask Ken to start a fire despite being warm. Looking at the cushions, I noticed they held no impressions. The fireplace was as clean as our kitchen floor. This room wasn't for living. It was to show wealth, impressing and humbling all who entered. I didn't know the term *conspicuous consumption;* however, in a college Economics class when I read of Thorsten Veblen, I thought of the Moseleys with their matching red Caddies and velvet settee. Ken now owns most of that furniture and the family tree hangs over his fireplace in his living room, although he chose not to live in the original Moseley mansion. He built his own near the Trion Country Club close to Mike and Jacob's sister Susan.

"You coming?" Ken asked.

"It's a bit much," Jacob would later tell me.

When Ken led us into the party room, "Green-Eyed Lady" by Sugarloaf was playing, and I've often wondered at the coincidence. Yes, my eyes are green. Did Mike put that song on when he heard the doorbell? He denies it. Still, I think he may be lying. The chatter that competed with the music died down, and everyone at the party, including my brother, quit talking to look at us. The only other time that I've felt the discomfort of that level of attention was when I taught my first college class.

Jacob squeezed my hand and Ken, like a good host, spoke first. "Well, now, we're all here," and the moment passed. People turned back to one another and started talking.

"Y'all want Coke," Ken asked.

"We can handle it ourselves," Jacob said.

Ken grinned, went over to his girlfriend Barbara Ragsdale, and put his arm around her waist. Tall, blonde, and head cheerleader, she never let Ken far out of her sight. He was a known flirt then and continues to be. He whispered something in her ear, and she gave me a what-are-you-looking-at glare. I did what Aunt Grace did when folks gave her the evil eye: smiled and kept looking. Barbara and I never liked each other. Still don't.

I recognized everybody at the party. Cindy Roberts, a varsity cheerleader with short red hair, was talking to Charlie Roden, the quarterback called Hunk. Touching shoulder to shoulder with Paul Evans, center and stereotypical jock, was Leann Cochran, the sexy star at Trion High. Drum majorette in the eleventh grade, built like Raquel Welch and proud of it, Leann always wore her sweaters a size too small. Then there was Mary Jane, Mike's girlfriend since the fifth grade. Nearly five-five with brown curly hair and a voice twice her size, she established herself as the queen bee early on. They were my superiors. The Moseley place was known for the best parties in Trion where Ken only entertained the in-group, and I knew I didn't belong. Yet there I was with the prince of the city.

Mike was standing near the stereo, thumbing through the records. We went in that direction.

"If it's not my sweet sister," he said. "What took y'all so long?"

"My fault," I said. "I always wanted to arrive at a party fashionably late."

"What's fashionable about being late?" he asked.

"We got to make our grand entrance," Jacob said. "I'll get those Cokes."

We watched Jacob walk away. Mike gave me a look, and I whispered, "He's been a perfect gentleman."

"He better," Mike said and headed over to the couch where Mary Jane sat by herself, looking pissed.

Jacob returned with two Cokes and Leann, her arm looped over his shoulder and her breast pressed against his arm.

"You're the lucky girl tonight," she said, still hanging on Jacob. "I'm surprised Mike didn't keep you away from danger."

Jacob handed me my Coke, untangled himself, and moved next to me. "Hush, Leann. You'll run the girl off."

"I can take care of myself," I said, rubbing my peace sign.

"Oh, my. We've a baby hippie in our midst." She smiled, turned, and waved over her shoulder. "Don't do anything I wouldn't do," Leann said and pranced back to Cindy and Charlie.

"Sorry about that," Jacob said. "She doesn't mean to be rude."

"Does she have a crush on you?"

"No. We're just friends. She's part of the gang," he said, taking a long swallow of his Coke. I got a whiff of something more than Coke: freshly cut hay. I knew that smell from Father's Jim Beam under the kitchen sink.

Mike put on "I'll Be There" by The Jackson 5.

"Want to dance?" Jacob asked.

"Here?"

"Why not?"

"I'm not very good."

"Neither am I."

I reached out, took his Coke, and drank. The whiskey burned, but I didn't cough. He took both bottles, put them on a table, and pulled me close. We swayed awkwardly until I reached up and draped my arms around his neck. His warmth spread through me. I started to perspire to the point of becoming damp and asked if we could step outside. The heat never left me, and I understood how some girls slipped into motherhood before graduation.

Like good southern boys and girls raised with proper manners, everyone behaved politely toward me. Even so, I did hear a few *bless her heart* and *well, I never would have guessed* and some other phrases I can't recall. I always imagined they thought it inappropriate that Jacob brought me, but Jacob being Jacob, they let it slide. Rocking to the beat of "Rubber Band Man" while Barbara and Leann went to powder their noses, Ken came toward us. Jacob intercepted him, saying my dance card was full.

Except Cindy, most of those girls never really became my friends. She later said that they all saw Jacob "falling hard" because he stayed by me the entire party. I wonder if he knew he was "falling hard" when I walked down those stairs at home.

By the end of that night, we were a couple. And we remained a couple. Eventually, he admitted straying once with Leann when he was drinking. I forgave him. I always forgave him because of who he was. I also left him because of who he was. I never remarried because no one else was Jacob. In truth, on our first date, I was Juliet with a touch of the shrewish Katherina. I guess I still am.

Thankfully the shades were drawn. Wrapped in a red kimono covered with intertwined gold serpents, Georgia looked down at me. Her hair damp from the shower and her breath fresh with the fragrance of Crest. I was naked and sticky.
—Jacob Hall, "Behold, I Give You the Power"

# Chapter 3

Moseley Funeral Home
Friday, September 13, 2019
Visiting Hours: 6:00-9:00 p.m.


The parking lot of the Moseley Funeral Home is unusually crowded for a viewing on football night. The cynic in me suspects many of these folks are here to see if time's worn down the golden boy in the way it's worn them down. Before dressing to come, I looked through some of our wedding pictures. We didn't have a professional photographer or caterer or wedding planner. Mother did most of the arranging with her friends who took pictures and baked sweets except for the three-tiered cake by Cross Bakery for the church reception. Aunt Grace provided the flowers that she and her neighbor Miss Irene picked in the countryside. Jacob and I look like babes, our skin smooth with no wrinkles, and our smiles wide, teeth still white. In the days before smoking and drinking take their toll, he appears particularly handsome. The last time I saw him, July in Illinois, his skin was sallow with lines creviced more by worry than sun. Hopefully, Ken can restore Jacob's younger appearance.

I can't shake the thought that I somehow killed him. Why else did I lie to Susan? My threat to cut him off might have been the last bit of stress that could cause his heart attack. Granted, Jacob's habits were also to blame, and the Halls aren't long-lived; nonetheless, it is incontrovertible that he was alive when we spoke and dead the next morning. In the eyes of the law, I'm not guilty. However, possibly I could be sued in a civil court for wrongful death.

*All the circumstantial evidence is piled in front as Susan's lawyer interrogates me.*

*Susan's lawyer: Please answer my questions with a yes or no. You divorced Jacob Hall on the grounds of irreconcilable differences?*

*Janet: Yes*

*Susan's lawyer: You continued to have sexual relations with Jacob.*

*Janet: Yes*

*Susan's lawyer: These relations continued while Jacob was engaged to his second wife.*

*Janet: Yes*

*Susan's lawyer: After they were married?*

*Janet: Yes*

*Susan's lawyer: While she was pregnant with his children?*

*Janet: Yes*

*Susan's lawyer: You sabotaged his marriage, didn't you?*

*Janet: No.*

*Susan's lawyer: How is that a legitimate answer?*

*Janet: I don't know. She slept with Jacob while we were married.*

*Susan's lawyer: Do you have proof?*

*Janet: No.*

*Susan's lawyer: Therefore, you have no defense.*

*Janet: I guess not.*

*Susan's lawyer: You admit guilt?*

*Janet: I didn't kill him.*

*Susan's lawyer: Didn't you? Would he be dead now if you had moved on? Made a clean break?*

*Janet: I don't know. Nobody knows.*

*Susan's lawyer: I think the jury knows.*


Mustering the courage to see Jacob for the last time, I stay in my car and listen to "Peace Train." I hear a knock. Cindy's at the window.

"Waiting for me?" she asks.

"For Jacob," I say, holding back tears. "We spent many a night making out in this parking lot."

"Strange place for horny teenagers," she says, opening my door.

"That's why we chose it. Jacob called it fucking with death."

"In more ways than one," she says.

"Exactly what he meant."

Sliding her arm through the crook of mine, Cindy leads me through the vehicles. This walk is the beginning of the end. If I just stayed in my blue Honda, maybe I could erase this moment and drive into the sunset with Jacob.

"Here we are," she says and opens the door to the funeral home.

I step over the threshold, my heel catching on the aluminum rise as if I may be refused entrance, prohibited from saying goodbye. The near fall makes the night all the more unbearable when I look up to see Jacob Hall, 1954-2019 in bold letters on the door to my right. White lilies with silver ribbon in a silver urn offer no comfort.

In a black suit and vest, Denny, Ken's assistant, holds the door open for us. Susan, her husband Larry, and their daughter Crystal stand next to a closed casket draped in a huge spray of red roses, buds more than half open and waiting for full bloom. Scattered among the flowers are sprigs of baby's breath and mock orange leaves. The coffin's reddish-brown mahogany reminds me of the time Jacob and I shopped for Aunt Grace's coffin. "Mahogany's feasible only if money's no object," Ken said. Married to an esteemed dentist, Susan wants Trion to witness their wealth even in death.

Standing in the line of traffic, neither Cindy nor I move. I see folks I've seen in town but don't know and others who're totally unfamiliar. Given Jacob's high school image and the Hall family's history in Trion, dating back to the 1850s, I'm not surprised by the numbers. The dark clothing and hushed tones of bereavement become a surreal painting turned nightmare. I'm on the verge of a panic attack, pulse speeding up and body flush.

"Why a closed casket?" Cindy asks.

"No clue."

"You okay?"

"Not really." I don't admit I'm having a panic attack. When Jacob's lying dead, it seems selfish to call attention to myself.

"We should pay our respects," Cindy says.

Mike and Mary Jane are talking to Susan. Crystal looks very adult in a black pants suit.

Cindy takes my arm and leads me down the center of the aisle to Jacob. With each step, I feel as if I'm about to pass out. We stop at the casket. Cindy chatters about the roses while I stare at the striations in the wood, trying to lose myself in the patterns. Maybe the head of a howling dog, eyes shut, or a hand grasping a branch, thumb and wrist exposed.

Cindy comes closer and whispers, "People are waiting." I don't move so she repeats louder, "People are waiting." Lifting my left hand, I kiss it and place my palm and fingers on the mahogany before pressing my body against the wood, arms reaching around. Somewhere in his velvet bed Jacob must feel my love and remorse.

Cindy tugs at my elbow, finally pulling me away, and we walk toward Susan. Wearing a black lace dress, scalloped around the shoulders, she appears the model of grief. In the back, Mike, Mary Jane, and the rest of Jacob's posse are leaving. Mike gives me a weak smile.

Mary Jane's normal glare seems softened by our shared grief. Checking my watch, I see that the Trion High School Aggies will start play in twenty minutes.

"So sorry for your loss," Cindy says and begins to talk to Larry while I offer condolence to Susan, who reaches out and hugs me.

She speaks softly in my ear, "I wish you were the one in that coffin."

"So do I."

After speaking to Larry and Crystal, Cindy joins the gang from high school, and I walk over to talk to Ken, who's watching the door. He bends, hugs me, and kisses my cheek. I hold on a little too long when he straightens up and steps back, still gazing at the door.

"Why the closed casket, Ken?"

Pausing for a minute, he adjusts his tie and suit coat. "Susan said Jacob is an organ donor."

"What's that got to do with anything?"

"Some think organ donations distort the deceased's body."

"I know for a fact it doesn't," I say. "Aunt Grace had an open casket."

"That's what Susan instructed me."

"You've seen the body. Was Jacob distorted?"

"Such information is confidential except for immediate family."

"I'm family."

"You were."

"Jacob never mentioned a closed casket."

Like most men his age, Ken dislikes being questioned and shifts from foot to foot, tugs at his jacket, and sweeps his hair back with his fingers. "Thanks for coming over, Janet. Don't forget to sign the registry," he says and walks over to greet his wife Barbara, leaving me by myself. I was married to Jacob for over ten years and slept with him for nearly fifty and have no rights. Disenfranchised, I join Cindy and the class of 1972 outside.

There they are. Cindy, Mike, Mary Jane, Leann, Charlie, and Paul huddled under the pecan tree, Dixie cups in hand, smoke rising from cigarettes once stashed in a purse or pocket or glove compartment despite the surgeon general's warning in 1964. "I'm taking death into my own hands," Jacob used to say when opening a new package of Marlboro Reds, those manly weeds of cowboy fame.

"Hey, sis," Mike says.

"I can use a drink," I reply.

Paul hands me a Dixie cup.

"Every girl wanted Jacob. I wouldn't have let him go," Leann says, handing her empty cup to Paul. Now her figure is a more voluptuous version of the former head majorette.

"The best looking, smartest, most caring guy in the world," Mary Jane says.

"Best looking?" Mike asks his wife, who punches his shoulder then kisses him.

"And smartest," Charlie says.

"No wonder you never remarried," Mary Jane says. "You couldn't find anybody better."

"The game's already started," Mike says. "You coming, sis?"

"I think I'll go back in and tarry a while."

"See you tomorrow," he says and leaves with Mary Jane's hand in his.

I don't like that bitch, but she loves my brother, and he loves her for some unfathomable reason. Cindy hugs me, and I know she'd stay here with me. I tell her I'll see her tomorrow.

Leann drops her cigarette to the ground and crushes it under her shoe. Paul and Charlie wait for her. She looks at me with vitriol, hate, disgust, anger all competing to overwhelm me.

"Why in the fuck did you leave him?"

"Hi," I said and reached for my vapor pen.

"You can't smoke in here."

"What time is it?"

"It's nine seventeen and you have twenty-three minutes to get showered and dressed. Your clothes are in the dryer," she said and gently squeezed my jaw, popped two aspirin in my mouth, and handed me the Coke in an old-fashioned returnable eight-ounce bottle. It was, and I know it is, a cliché, the best thing I've ever drunk. Bristling with energy and impatience, Georgia stood above me.

—Jacob Hall, "Behold, I Give You the Power"

# Chapter 4

Moseley Funeral Home
Friday, September 13, 2019
Visiting Hours: 6:00 to 9:00 p.m.

Why in the fuck did I leave him?

It wasn't a big event like a hurricane traveling up from the Gulf and dumping fourteen inches of rain in a couple of hours, flooding everyone at the base of Sand Mountain. Our marriage eroded, bit by bit. I started to change. Jacob stayed Jacob.

When we began our life together, I was a girl, barely old enough for a driver's permit. I could sit behind the steering wheel and drive only if someone with a license sat next to me in the passenger seat. That was Jacob. He was the adult, the one who knew how to steer. Gently, never raising his voice, he taught me how to maneuver. And I was an attentive student, listening to his every word.

Jacob stayed in Trion and went to CC while I finished high school. Four months after graduating, I married him, and, side by side, we left Trion for Tuscaloosa and the University of Alabama. He was a junior in English, and I was a freshman just like when we started dating. We both received scholarships and lived in subsidized married-student housing. Jacob taught me the ropes of being an English major. I kept house, he wrote, and we studied. He recognized that we each had jobs, though he thought his more important, the holy of holies: the creation of the written word. When he graduated, the M.F.A. program gave him a full ride while I finished my B.A. We were awarded our U.A.T. degrees the same day.

The University of South Carolina was one of the few Ph.D. programs with a creative writing track. Jacob received another full scholarship as I started my M.A. in literature. We lived in married-student apartments, and our life at first was much like that in Tuscaloosa. Study and keep house, study and write. Then we found ourselves in the same classes, equals in the eyes of the professors and students. I can't say that I competed with Jacob; I can't say that I didn't. What I discovered was that I no longer needed him to show me the way.


Columbia, South Carolina
Thursday, March 25, 1982
3:30 p.m.


We'd just gotten out of our Whitman-Dickinson seminar. "Want a beer or a walk in the park?" Jacob asked.

"Let's do both," I said.

We picked up a Miller quart at the 7-Eleven and poured it in our red plastic traveling cups. Riverfront Park was just a few blocks from the university. Tall oaks lined the towpath of the old Columbia Canal, with benches near open spaces where we could sit or pitch a blanket and watch Frisbees spinning in air. A young boy, nine or ten, played fetch with a Golden Lab. He hurled the ball, and the dog chased it at full speed, braking too late and skidding past us, then turning and scooping up the tennis ball before trotting back with head held high, emitting a low growl.

"We should get a dog," Jacob said. I thought of the work that came with a canine: house training him not to pee on the rug, taking him out for walks, being waked early to feed him, entertaining him with throw animals, and teaching him not to chew the furniture.

"Too much work," I said.

"What do you mean?"

"I'll be the one walking him, feeding him, cleaning up after him. You'll toss him a toy."

Jacob put his arms around me, snuggling closer. Lifting my hair, he kissed my neck.

"You suggest a project for us, like growing tomatoes, and I'm the one left digging and fertilizing and watering and staking the vines."

"A dog would be different. He would be ours."

"Tomatoes are ours."

"You eat more," Jacob said.

I punched him. "Don't be an asshole."

He smiled and rubbed his arm.

"No, Jacob. We'd pick him out, bring him home, and you'd go back to your writing 'til after midnight. It's too much."

"Too much?"

"I'm always tending to us."

"Don't I help?"

"Not enough."

He moved away and looked at me, then lowered his eyes as if he were hurt, as if I'd accused him of something but he wasn't sure what.

"I cook, I clean. You hole up with your writing."

"Look at that Golden Lab," Jacob said.

"You look," I said.

"Wouldn't he be fun?"

"For you, maybe. I don't want a dog."

Like two strangers, we sat looking into space without uttering a word.

I spoke first. "I've always been somebody's kid or your girlfriend. Now I'm in grad school. I'm finding myself."

"What does that mean, Janet?"

"I want to teach literature, maybe get a Ph.D. I'm tired of being the caretaker."

"Didn't I take care of you in high school?" he asked.

"Yes."

"Didn't I get you out of Trion?"

"I was young then. I want to take care of myself now."

"We're in this together," he said.

"Exactly. We're partners," I said.

We watched the Lab, who wanted to fetch again, prance in front of the boy, who attached the leash. They walked away.

"I love you, Janet," Jacob said.

"Let's go home," I said.

We were three blocks up the hill and one block off University Drive. Our apartment had one back bedroom, one bathroom, and a small kitchen with a counter dividing it from the front room. An old sofa bed took up most of the space. It had belonged to Jacob's folks, who'd upholstered it twice., first with a nubby yellow material, then a burgundy cotton bought at the textile outlet near Trion. When we moved to Columbia, his parents gave us the sofa bed that barely fit in the U-Haul.

With his writing, Jacob pretty much took over the apartment. Starting in the bed, he'd write longhand, propping a yellow legal pad on his knees, tossing crumpled paper all over the bed sheets. At noon, he'd rise out of the scrunchy balls, stretch, hit the bathroom, grab a

Coke, and return to writing in our bed. Usually he was writing, thinking about writing, talking about writing, and/or working on another draft of his writing. He'd write a short story, maybe twenty pages, type draft after draft, hang them all, page by page, on a clothesline he'd strung in the living room, often running several lines parallel. When the new draft went up, the old one came down, like black and white prayer flags changed whenever the last version was ready. Walking through the pages, I felt trapped in Hitchcock's *The Birds*, perched and waiting. I frequently escaped to the library where I had a carrel all to myself and began to wonder if marriage actually prepares us to be alone.

As soon as we walked in from the park, Jacob took my hand and led me to the bedroom. He closed the shades and slipped my T-shirt over my head, dropping it to the floor. Before unzipping my jeans and pulling them down with my underwear, he pulled his own shirt off. When he lay me on the sheets, I was warm and pulled him in, lifting my hips. That day I held myself back. His hands coiled around me until I released the expected scream, the signal to let himself finish. While sleep consumed him, I lay in twilight. When I came back from the bathroom, he was snoring. I left a note on the dresser: *Gone to the library. Back by 10. Love you. PS Still no dog.*


Moseley Funeral Home
Friday, September 13, 2019
Visiting Hours: 6:00-9:00 p.m.


Except for Susan, who sits in the front row, the viewing room is empty. Ken and Barbara have gone to the game, as have Larry and Crystal. I sit down next to Susan.

"Sorry about earlier," she says.

"That's okay."

I want to ask why the casket is closed, but Susan's face is a mess. Tears have destroyed her mascara. She waves away my offer of a Kleenex. This loss of vanity is unnatural for the Susan I've always known—hair styled in Birmingham and "face work" done in Atlanta. She couldn't show her grief in a more profound way.

"When I was four," Susan begins, "our great grandmother Ann, on Mama's side, passed away. Her body lay for two days in our home for friends and family to view. Mama and Dad sat with the body all night both nights and sent Jacob and me upstairs to bed. Did he ever tell you about this?"

"He did," I answer and start to reach for her hand.

Clutching the bag in her lap, she says, "We used to honor the deceased more in those days."

"There were a lot of folks here tonight paying respect," I say.

"It was just a pre-game show for many going to the Bama-Gamecock game in Columbia tomorrow."

"Those who really knew Jacob will stay for his funeral."

For the first time since I sat down, Susan looks at me. Her anger is obvious. She blames me for taking Jacob away, for the infrequent visits after we married, even after we split. This is not a good time to ask if I can see him. There never will be.

"How could anybody really know Jacob? He left Trion so young."

Susan's question feels like a stab.

"Can I see him?" I ask.

She stands, tidies her dress, pulls out a compact, and repairs her makeup.

"Can I see Jacob?" I ask again.

"No," she says.

"Please."

"No. I don't want anyone to see the man who's gone—the ruins of him. I want everyone to remember the boy you took away," she says and walks out.

I stay with him, sealed in mahogany and covered with flowers, and wonder how I can open the coffin when I hear a polite cough and see Denny at the door. Given that Ken's two daughters aren't interested in this business, Denny's calm posture and pleasant demeanor suggest that Ken has found the man eventually to take his place.


Columbia, South Carolina
Sunday, December 14, 1980
2:00 p.m.


Jacob was on the phone with Susan. She'd called, as she often did on Sunday after church. I lay on the couch, pretending to read *Wuthering Heights* for next semester's British Romanticism Seminar as I eavesdropped. From Jacob's monosyllabic answers, I guessed Susan was pushing for us to stay with her instead of Aunt Grace. After he said he loved her and would call soon, Jacob hung up. But he kept looking at the phone as if the news was its fault.

I put my book down, went to the fridge, and got us each a beer.

"Tell me," I said.

"Susan wants us to spend the week after Christmas with Larry and her."

"That's nearly two weeks there. Almost all of our winter vacation."

He drank and I watched as he rephrased Susan's arguments into his own.

"We can spend more time with friends."

"Your friends."

"Not yours?"

"Charlie, Paul, and Ken are your high school buddies. I'm included because I'm with you. Same as in high school."

"They're all married."

I gave him my best withering look. "We can discuss decorating, kids, the club, and the differences between Faulkner and Hemingway."

"It's not my fault you didn't make friends."

"I started dating you and we lived in your world. I didn't mind, but they were your friends."

"What's your problem?"

I counted to ten in my head. Jacob was shifting into good-ole-boy mode where he expected me to be the girl.

"No problem. Just following your advice—'small towns are for the small-minded.'"

"Janet, I don't want to live there, but Trion folks are good folks."

"Neither do I. I also don't want to spend our entire break in Trion. A week is enough."

"Okay. Can we at least stay at Susan's?"

I left the room and came back holding Molly Bloom, our fat brown tabby who, I was convinced, was part Maine Coon because of her eighteen-pound size and the tufts of hair on the tips of her ears. "Is Molly Bloom invited?"

"You know the answer."

"If I don't bring the cat, we'll have to split our stay with Mike and Mary Jane. I can't take two weeks of living with Susan and Mary Jane."

We both took a drink from our beers. I imagined Jacob was going to try a different argument. In the past I would have been more anxious to please. Graduate school had given me a boost in confidence and a desire to be more than Jacob's wife, which I still was to almost everyone in Trion. The lucky girl who caught the golden ring.

"You never tried to fit in."

"You're saying I'm a snob."

"What did you do other than play drums in the band?"

"Studied. Read. Dreamed of getting out."

"That's what I mean."

"You never mentioned my aloofness then."

"No. I found it intriguing. But I wanted acceptance, too. You didn't seem to give a damn."

"Oh, I did. And you had both. Brains and popularity. I just couldn't swallow my pride and play Barbie for a world of Barbies and Kens."

"But I did play Ken?"

"Somehow you managed without sacrificing that beautiful brain."

"We're talking high school. We're in grad school now."

"Most of those Trionites are still living those days. It's a world we left, and I don't even want to visit except to see my kin."

"Can we stay a few extra days if we stay at Grace's?"

I nodded. And then Jacob did what he always did when we had friction. He fucked me 'til I came. Afterwards, I daydreamed that Aunt Grace had a beautiful guest room as did Susan and Mike instead of an air mattress on her study floor.

"Where's my car?"

"Back at the County Line. Now get in the shower." She started to pull the covers off the bed. I held on and she laughed, "Come on, Professor. I saw every inch of you last night and kissed a fair portion of it too." She looked at her watch. "You got twenty minutes. I'll make you an egg sandwich. You can eat it on the way."

—Jacob Hall, "Behold, I Give You the Power"

# Chapter 5

The Williams House
Friday, September 13, 2019
10:00 p.m.

On the gravel driveway, I sit in the car and look at my house: small, single-story, two bedrooms, one bath, and a free-standing garage that contains most of my belongings from Columbia except for books, clothes, electronics, and a few dishes that I unpacked. This little red-brick house in a town where I don't want to live is what I've traded for Jacob, the love of my life, my best friend, and once my mentor. When we were young, we talked about the future like looking into a crystal ball. He wanted to write, I wanted to learn, and we both wanted to be with each other. No happier existence could we imagine until he desired kids and I desired independence. Instead of a partner, I'd begun to feel like a housewife, a fate I would never embrace. He never saw himself as the conventional husband with a wife to care for him. He never quite understood what I meant about finding myself and why I had to leave him. In the divorce, those back-and-forth months, I discovered that neither of us was able to let go the umbilicus of passion.

I wanted him back here to make the place more bearable for me. Us against the world. It was that way in the beginning. It could be that way in the end. He could choose to return to Trion or lose me. The stress of my threat pushed him over the edge. Did he have high blood pressure or heart disease? I'm not sure. We rarely discussed such things. We were still locked in where we were: talking about writing—his—and literature and teaching—mine—and, when together, fucking like teenagers. Maybe he used Viagra; he never said. I'm on hormones and have no other health issues except the body's slow decay that is the destiny of us all. "Age appropriate" according to the doctors. Jacob continued to smoke and drink like a graduate student. At least I quit smoking cigarettes.

No longer the ingenue, I took some pleasure in gaining control: his dependence, his failing confidence, his near paralysis. My approval was more important to him than being published. Or so he said. If I could speak to him again, I'd apologize for my wrongdoing. Let him hear my sorrow. I have to see him. Just one more time, a chance to ask Jacob to forgive me, one last chance to say how much I truly love him. Ken needs to open the coffin, and I text him.

```
Call me.
I can't. Barbara's ready for bed.
Please.
Get some sleep. Tomorrow's a long day.
Call me when you get to work.
Will do. The tribute was moving.
```

Useless to text him again. I hear his determination. Checking my other texts, I see one from Cindy asking if I'm home and another from Mike saying the tribute went well. How could it not? Jacob was a great guy, loved by almost everyone who ever met him. His crooked smile and strong handshake pulled folks close to him no matter the occasion. Mother used to say his affection was dangerous. From the beginning, I adored him. He had a sweetness I've never witnessed in another man. My dear brother Mike, as accommodating as he is, doesn't exude Jacob's compassion. He was unconditionally sympathetic. He loved people, loved animals, and he loved the earth.

I walk into the study and dig through stacks of literary journals with Jacob stories, finally finding his first published story, still one of my favorites, "The Land," in *The Georgia Review*: "Poor people only have their family and human dignity. They can't even call the land their own." When I first read these words, I cried. They are so Jacob. Full of heart and empathy for those the rich try to crush. Reading through it again, I hear his voice—gravelly, gritty, a little raspy with a slight drawl. I especially loved it when he'd roll over in the middle of the night and say, "I love you, baby."

Scrolling through my emails, I discover his story, "Behold, I Give You the Power." Like much of his early writing, this piece examines the Protestant passion of the rural South, folks who look for signs that they're God's chosen. As I read, I feel the chill of Jacob's early words that often seem like wind blowing through him. The young Jacob isn't as worried about books and prizes, about being somebody in a literary world. He wants to convey what he perceives is the mystery of life. When he ages and gains more experience, his writing becomes more controlled, polished, complex syntax with clause after clause replacing fragments and short phrases strung together with a plethora of *ands*. His words become more deliberate and thoughtful. He becomes Faulknerian. Perhaps this change in style that was always his goal has grown archaic in a contemporary world where most of the editors are young. Jacob's older, white-male voice has fallen from favor, no longer given the privileged treatment as it was in his youth. Today's young editors support younger and more diverse voices.

Rhoda walks in and meows. I pick her up, grab a handful of treats, and take her to bed. She's fussier than usual and deserts me for the closet. I fantasize fetching a crowbar from the garage and breaking into Jacob's coffin then driving away with his body like a character in some movie I once saw. Finally, my eyes shut. Tossing from one side to the other, I see Jacob walk out of gray clouds, his body covered in granules of silvery charcoal.


The Williams House
Saturday, September 14, 2019
7:30 a.m.


The sun pushes through the curtains. Rhoda pulls on the sheet and pricks the cotton with her sharp claws. She's hungry, and I shoo her away. Ten pounds of feline stubbornness, she positions herself on my chest, purring so loudly that I finally open my eyes to her big green orbs and give her some dry food from my bedside drawer. I know. Feeding her in bed is letting her ruin my sleep plus scattering Purina pellets on the sheet. Yet it's only the two of us, most of the time.

At the foot of my bed on the wall is an eight-by-twelve-inch watercolor Jacob painted in college: a Standard Oil station with a neon Coca-Cola sign and a teenager in overalls at the door. Next to it is a picture of William Faulkner in a light jacket, arms crossed, his right hand cupping the bowl of his pipe, and his head turned slightly to the left. "His dark eyes see what few can ever see," Jacob once said when he handed me *As I Lay Dying*. I often wonder what Mr. Faulkner would see in me lying on this bed. Would he see a crone and her cat surrounded by books? Or would he see me at eighteen in the picture with Jacob taken the night after our wedding? Shoulder-length brown hair and green eyes, I wore a mid-calf, white, rayon dress with covered buttons up the front. Jacob, clean shaven at twenty, had brown curls and brown eyes. He wore a white Oxford shirt, rolled to his elbows, and a pair of khakis. Probably the happiest day of my life—September 15, 1974. Drinking arms linked, we're each holding a glass of champagne.

Tomorrow would be our forty-fifth wedding anniversary had we stayed married. The appropriate gift: blue sapphire, signifying spiritual clarity and romantic love. We would have exchanged books. Books are where we started. Reading and the love of language united and sustained us. And we loved each other passionately. But we couldn't hold a marriage together on passion — for each other and for words. He never outgrew the traditional habit of husband and wife. I understand why he couldn't put me above his writing. I didn't understand why he couldn't place me on a par with it. I resented being second and made him pay with his life. Illinois is not Antarctica. I could have sold Aunt Grace's house and moved to be with Jacob. Who would I have left behind? Cindy, Clara, and Mike.

The wood floor feels cool as I walk barefoot, following Rhoda to the kitchen. She springs from one side to the other in the direction of the refrigerator. With her early scratching and bouncing, Rhoda's almost as annoying as my father used to be with his "Up and at 'em." However, today is different. I need Rhoda to show me life will go on without Jacob. I scrape the tuna from the can and spoon it into her bowl before patting the fish into a mound that my spoiled kitty eats from the inside out, leaving a hole in the center like a small volcano pit.

Expecting Mike to drop by, I make a full pot of coffee: six tablespoons of Maxwell House that I let Mr. Coffee take over, gurgling and hissing while dripping into the pot. After filling my mug, I reach for whole milk then put it back, remembering Jacob drank his coffee black unless he had a hangover. "Caffeine's a cheap high. This stuff trips you for hours," he'd say. And he was right, as he often seemed to be when we were first together.

In his faded Neil Young T-shirt, cradling his mug with both hands, he'd sit across the table from me, his dark hair matted on the right where he'd slept. I could hear the soft hiss of his breath as he blew on the hot liquid, air puffing his cheeks, his lips nearly vibrating like someone playing a trumpet. I loved them especially the bottom lip, full with a cheeky little quirk in the corner. Even at fifteen I wanted to bite it. I could sit for hours, listening to him read a new story, his voice unsure the words wanted him there, waiting for them to high five and skedaddle. He cleared his throat often, giving them space, and then would stop reading altogether, toss his pages to the side, and grab me around the waist.

I hear Mike's Ford pickup in the driveway. Forever a clean freak and more so after his two-year stint in the Army, he runs that truck through the car wash every Wednesday and Saturday. The glint off the white hood suggests that he's already taken it through. I watch him take off his MAGA hat and stow it behind the seat before stepping out.

"Still in your bathrobe," he quips, walking through the back door and pouring himself a cup. Rhoda heads back to the bedroom, her tail up in the air. He doesn't take to indoor pets, and she doesn't take to men. I move a stack of freshman essays to the counter.

"You should've joined us at the game last night," he says.

"I was wiped out after the visitation. What did you say about Jacob at halftime?"

"Best brother-in-law, always gave me his tickets for Bama home games."

"Jacob lost interest in football after he left Trion," I say.

"I was glad he did."

"What did the other guys say?"

"Ken said Jacob never let his friends down. His word good as gold."

"That was true, most of the time," I say.

"Paul said he was always ready to help. And Charlie called Jacob the smartest man he ever knew. Then we prayed."

"Jacob would've been touched. He loved you guys."

"We loved each other, still do. Those were good times."

"We were young and full of hope," I say.

"Why do you think Susan scheduled his funeral on a football Saturday? Why not a weekday?" Mike asks.

"Jacob's girls are in school, his colleagues at Illinois State are still teaching. Plus today is an away game for Bama."

"I never think about folks having to travel far for a Trion funeral," Mike says, looking back down at his phone. "Why was his casket closed?"

"I've no idea about that. Susan said she wanted us to remember the boy who left, not the man he was."

"Really? We've all seen him since he left," Mike says, scrolling down the messages on his phone.

"He wanted to be cremated, ashes scattered in the air," I say.

"I'm surprised you two never moved to California," Mike says. "You are wearing a dress today."

"I'm wearing a black pants suit, the one I wore to Aunt Grace's funeral."

"Janet, girls here don't dress like tomboys. Girls wear dresses."

"I'm a woman, Mike, not a girl, and what I wear is my choice."

"This is not some university town."

"Aunt Grace hardly ever wore a dress," I say.

"Yeah. And everybody thought she was a tomboy, especially with that short hair and no makeup."

"Mike, the term is lesbian."

"Don't say that about our aunt."

"Nothing wrong with being a lesbian. Your wife watches 'Ellen.'"

"Leave Mary Jane out of it. Anyway, this is Alabama. Not the land of fruits and nuts."

"The land of rednecks and guns."

Glaring at him, I squeeze my mug. I rarely, if ever, agree with him. I haven't agreed with Mike since I was old enough to form my own opinions. Like me, he was grown on the mountain; unlike me, my brother never shook the sand off his shoes. After high school he went to Baptist College in Birmingham, sixty miles southwest, and drove home every weekend to see Mary Jane, his high-school girlfriend. There's something about first sweethearts that I understand. What I love about my brother has more to do with the past than the present.

"Want to drive me around while I run some errands for Susan?" I ask.

"Sure. Where?"

"The Lunch Box for pimento cheese sandwiches and Heavenly Baked Goods for brown butter chocolate chip cookies."

"Why not peanut butter?"

"I'll buy those for your funeral."

"Don't hold your breath. Fit as a fiddle," he says, extending his right arm and tightening his biceps. "And you can't eat cookies at your own funeral."

"Not bad for somebody who sits on his butt and shuffles money all day," I say.

He looks at my walls and cabinets. "Thought you were going to spruce up this place and put it on the market."

This kitchen is the way Aunt Grace wanted it in the mid-1950s: pale yellow walls, turquoise shelves with glass-paneled doors, and a red chrome kitchen table edged in aluminum with two blue-gray chairs from the original eight.

"I like the colors."

"If you're living yesterday," Mike replies.

"You think Trion is a twenty-first century town? Annual Miss Slick Chick Contest before the Bear Bryant Barbeque? How long's he been dead?"

"Come off it. We're talking houses, and I know what sells."

"Not sure I'm ready," I tell him.

"When did you change your mind?"

"This last year Jacob and I talked about his moving in with me when he retired. He wasn't sure he could handle coming back."

"A lot of folks do," Mike said. "Family and friends are a real draw."

"Plus, I own this house, and he could have had all of me to himself." I smile.

"That idea's dead," Mike says.

Fighting the tears, I rub my eyes and lift my head. Mike's checking his iPhone again, thumbs clicking.

"Sorry," he says.

"Everything's unsettled now," I say.

"Better decide while prices are still good."

"What do you mean?"

"Everybody's moving to Lakeport."

"White flight?"

"The Supermercado on West Main sells more groceries than the Piggly Wiggly," he answers.

"The Latinx make this town finally interesting."

"Not to most folks around here," he says.

"Don't know if I want some stranger living in Aunt Grace's house."

"I would've sold it in a skinny minute."

"Maybe that's why she left it to me."

"Shame you weren't here to take care of her."

"I'm sorry I wasn't," I say, thinking about those dark months when I could only come on weekends and wanted to quit my job and move in with her, but she insisted I stay put.

I begin to cry. Mike walks over and puts his arms around me, leans his head down against mine. "We'll get through. Now let's run those errands." This is the Mike I loved growing up, the big brother who carried me on his shoulders when my feet were tired, who took his baby sister with him to the movies.

I slip into my gray sweats and climb into Mike's truck. No dust on the dash or touchscreens, no Coke cans or junk mail on the floor. His truck is cleaner than my house. "Born Country" by Alabama fills the cab. Jacob loved this band and particularly this song, yet when he moved to the Midwest, he rarely returned to Trion. I visited more frequently, often spending Christmas here, and always brought Rhoda and before her Molly Bloom so I could stay with Aunt Grace. Mike doesn't allow indoor pets. His hunting dogs live behind the garage in a kennel, and Mary Jane will never let a cat near her pristine Thomasville sofa and chairs. When Aunt Grace was dying, Mike cared for her and resents that she didn't leave her place to him.

"Did you eat any breakfast?" he asks.

"Not really."

"How about a sausage biscuit from Hardee's?"

I rub my stomach, feeling the slight roll under my sweats. When I was young, I watched my weight almost to the point of obsession. But no more. With age I enjoy eating, refusing to see it as an enemy.

Turning left on Highway 431, Mike heads to the site of Sand Mountain's original Hardee's on George Wallace Drive. Built in 1974, the year I graduated from Trion High, Hardee's has been remodeled five times.

"Their biscuits are still the best. I just don't like this mod building," Mike says, pulling in front of black tile with a single row of yellow tiles beneath the roof, the yellow matching Hardee's happy-face star edged in red. "Why don't people leave well enough alone? Nothing was wrong with brown brick and the orange Hardee's sign."

"Things change. They always change."

"Not everybody likes change," Mike says.

"Let's eat in the truck."

"Not in mine."

The place is half full. A young Latinx family leaving with their meals passes us, and Mike holds the door.

"Gracias," the mother says.

"You're welcome," Mike says.

Several tables are occupied by Latinx and whites of various ages and genders, all except one person staring at their cell phones. An older white couple sit next to each other in a booth near the door. I recognize them, though can't recall their names. Mike walks over to say hello, and I wave before stepping up to the cash register where a teenage girl with substantial makeup smiles and says, "What can I do for you, ma'am?" Her lipstick's Crimson Tide red, and her nails are painted Auburn orange and blue.

"I'd like the sausage, egg, and cheese biscuit without the egg and a diet coke without ice. Small," I say.

Mike joins me. "I'm easy. I want two sausage and egg biscuits and a large Coke."

"My treat." I hand the cashier a credit card.

As usual, Mike chooses a booth facing the door, a lesson he learned while watching *Maverick* on the parents' black and white GE television. He's almost done with his first biscuit when I slide in. My biscuit takes longer because it's a "special order."

"Thought you liked eggs," he says.

Waiting to see if he comments on what he's just said, I grin, and he stares at me, squeezing his lips together in annoyance.

"It's fresher when it doesn't stand prepared under those food lights," I say as steam rises from my biscuit.

Shaking his head, he smiles. "Early in our marriage, Mary Jane made me watch this chick flick, *When Harry Met Sally*. You're a lot like Sally. You want the world to arrange itself around you. But Trion is never going to change for you."

"Trion's changed already," I say with a full mouth. "When we were growing up, there were, what, ten thousand people. Now the population is closer to twenty thousand and not all of us look like you. Or me."

"I wish they did."

"Do you miss the Klan in white robes and hoods collecting money on 431 or that sign the Klan planted at the city limits?"

Mike takes another gulp from his Coke and shakes his head.

"It's never going be what it was," I say. "Change is inevitable."

"Is this how you lecture your students?"

"Kinda."

"You should still sell the house."

"Are you trying to get rid of me?"

"Doctor West tells me my blood pressure's high. I'm supposed to try to avoid stress."

I toss my napkin at him, and he catches it midair because he knows it's coming. He smiles, I laugh. He finishes his biscuit.

"I'm going to get a refill. Want me to top yours off?" he asks.

"Thanks."

I watch him and marvel at how precise he always is, filling each cup just below the top so the new lid fits without pressing out any of the liquid. Then he inserts clean straws and finally wraps each cold drink in a napkin so the cup won't sweat onto the immaculate surfaces of his Ford F-150. If only to annoy him, part of me wants to tell him about the ecological damage of plastic straws; however, I need Mike today. I have to bury Jacob.

Georgia wore a faded, yellow, cotton dress with small red flowers, tight and stretched in all the expected places. I imagined she'd bought the dress when she weighed about eight pounds less. Her blonde hair was held back by a black hair band. Her complexion was clear, and her face just beginning to succumb to gravity and the sun. Her earrings were small hoops—two on the right and one on the left. I don't remember any other piercings. She might have a tramp stamp of a honeysuckle vine, but I was too embarrassed by my drunken blackout to ask. I was hoping to find out later.

—Jacob Hall, "Behold, I Give You the Power"

# Chapter 6

Trion, Alabama
Saturday, September 14, 2019
8:30 a.m.

Mike likes to drive on the highway, and I don't. With uncontrolled access, 431 is like bumper cars at the fair. You never know when a vehicle will pull in front of you. I notice a red and white banner across the double doors of Roberts Furniture Store: *Relocated at 436 Gilley Road, Lakeport*. Roberts is one of those stores that constantly offers a going-out-of-business sale, so I'm not sure how to take this announcement.

"Has Roberts really closed its doors in Trion?" I ask.

"Yep. Two weeks ago."

"Why?"

"Why do you think? If you want to sell your house, you better do it now."

I get tired of hearing how brown people are running whites out of town.

"Los Arcos is doing a lot more breakfast business than Hardee's," I say as Mike stops at the light. He looks over at the sand-colored building and mumbles something under his breath. Like other older Trionites, he feels threatened by a shifting population. Aging whites refuse to remove the Confederate monument in front of the Davis County Courthouse, seated in Trion, and continue to fly the Confederate flag there. One day, possibly in their lifetime, they will be the minority, a future that Mike and many of his friends don't want to imagine.

"Where's the Hall family plot?" he asks.

"Near Mother's."

"It's been thirty years since she passed, and I still miss her every day," he says.

"I loved her a lot, but you know Aunt Grace felt more like my own mama. I told her everything, and she listened without judging."

"Ever visit her grave?" Mike asks.

"Whenever the spirit moves me. I planted two azalea bushes there. She loved azaleas."

"What about Mama and Dad?"

"I've been to Mother's plot a handful of times since moving back. Never to his," I say, readjusting my seatbelt.

"They're right next to each other," Mike says, stopping at another traffic light. "Do you stay long?"

"Long enough to leave her a potted plant."

"You remember how she'd take us to her parents' graves after Sunday church and sit there crying," he says.

"I don't remember that."

"Yeah, you do."

"No, I don't. Was Father there?"

"Never. Maybe we dropped him at home," Mike says.

"He was never nice to her," I say.

"Well, not by the time you grew up. He just got worse every year."

"I couldn't stand next to him without flinching when he made a sudden move."

Mike reaches over and takes my hand. Knowing how he and Aunt Grace were the only ones in the family who stood up for me, I feel myself on the verge of tears. Father's big gnarly hand flew into my cheek by habit, leaving red and blue marks. With Mother's pancake makeup I tried to cover the bruises though I could never hide them from Aunt Grace who confronted Mother who always denied it and defended him. Then Aunt Grace confronted him, he took a swing at her, and she filed assault charges against him. A sympathetic judge dismissed the case, and she never spoke to her brother again. After I turned fifteen and spent most of my time with Jacob, Father left me alone. Barely spoke to me. When I told Jacob about the slaps and beltings, he vowed to kill him if he ever touched me again.

Mike pulls up to The Lunch Box, with its little footballs painted all over the windows with a *Go Aggies* banner in black and red across the front. Like most places in the state, Trion was in love with its football team, named the Aggies because Trion High was originally a state agricultural school built in 1894. Every Friday night, the town moves to the field where most of the school board money is spent. A kid's name

40

is never mentioned without their team position or place in the band or on the cheering squad. The Aggies went to the state tournament once — 1971, Mike and Jacob's senior year. Mike, broad chested, was center and Jacob, wiry and fast, was a defensive back. I was a sophomore and played snare drums in the varsity band until Jacob and Mike graduated. Then I quit the band, never having been interested in football and all the social hoopla around it.

"I've got a couple of phone calls to make," Mike said.

Knowing Leann will be less of a bitch if Mike's there, I want him to go with me. Yet I don't want to ask and head in by myself. I've never cared for Leann, who owns The Lunch Box. Head majorette three years straight, she strutted like a Rockette and ran the majorettes, even called them "my girls," according to Jacob. He said they were afraid of her. She was too bossy, telling "her girls" how to manage their hygiene and looks, whom to date, and who was an acceptable friend. When I quit the band, I was not friend material unless I was with Jacob.

Open only for lunch, the restaurant has one room with a low ceiling and tables for four, spread with scarlet red-and-white-checkered tablecloths, Aggie colors. On each table is a single-flower glass vase. No orange or blue in The Lunch Box. No crimson red. Leann's smart enough not to show sides. The walls are framed with pictures of Trion High football teams and marching bands. Displayed prominently are the 1971 team, band, and cheerleaders because that's the year she graduated. Back then she looked like Dolly Parton's younger sister; however, she hasn't aged with the costly cosmetic miracles of Dolly. Closer to the picture, I find my sixteen-year-old self behind my snare. As usual, I'm not smiling.

Leann sits at one of the tables in the front, filling and sorting salt shakers, dropping in white rice to prevent sticking. Wearing floral cotton pants and a yellow flouncy blouse, low enough to divert attention to her breasts and away from her stomach, she has shoulder-length, bleached hair with a slight flip popular when she was eighteen. Cherry red veneers her lips and bleeds at the corners. Her lashes are coated black, casting a clumpy look. I take some satisfaction that I look at least ten years younger than Leann, voted sexiest her senior year.

I know she hears me come in, door scraping across linoleum. But she continues to work on her salt shakers.

"Morning," I say.

"Well, well, well. To what do I owe this honor?" she says, looking up.

"Sandwiches for Susan."

"Bless your heart for picking them up."

She sashays to the kitchen, her butt swinging side to side reminding me of high school when she strutted whenever she walked—down the hall, into class, or onto the field. She never seemed short of confidence, and it bothers me that she still can intimidate me as she did almost fifty years ago.

I remember one morning after homeroom when I was at my locker, Leann walked up.

"Why don't you try out for majorette next week?"

"That's not me," I said.

"You're too cute to play drums."

"What do you mean?"

"Tomboys play drums. I bet your aunt played drums. Anyway, Jacob probably would like to see you a majorette."

"How would you know what Jacob would like?"

"I know what boys like. You'll learn unless you're a tomboy."

Leann brings out two trays, each with three layers of triangled white bread, crusts cut off, and seeping pimento cheese on saran wrap. She hands them to me, and I dig my heels into the linoleum with each step to the front. "Me and Jacob had some fine times," she says as I close the door.

"That woman's a bitch. She was a bitch in high school, and she's still a bitch," I say after slamming the truck door.

"Watch your mouth, Janet. What would Jesus say?"

"He'd say 'Bless her heart. Leann is a bitch.'"

"What did she say this time?" he asks.

"Something about Jacob and her. I never see that bitch without her mentioning the two of them."

"Why do you care? You're the one he married."

"You'd get worked up too if some bruiser said Mary Jane fucked him."

"I'd know he was lying," Mike says.

"How?"

"Mary Jane is a goody two-shoes. She wouldn't sleep with me 'til we married."

"A lot of girls used to play virgin."

"Play?"

"Pretend they'd never done it so they could catch a nice husband."

"Not Mary Jane. Anyway, Trion's small enough I would've known."

"What about those summers she went to camp in Nashville?"

"You're a troublemaker, Janet. Anyway, that was long ago. I need to stop at the pharmacy," he says.

Columbia, South Carolina
Thursday, December 18, 1980
11:30 p.m.


Leann always flirted with Jacob, rubbing against him even when I was around. Once I thought I saw Jacob pat her butt.

"Why would I do that when I'm with you?" he asked.

I was too naïve and infatuated to entertain the thought of his sleeping with her and me at the same time. He was one of the good ones. Six years after our marriage, we'd drunk nearly a bottle of Jim Beam when he confessed—or so I thought. After turning in grades and lying on the floor beside the fireplace, he began kissing and licking my neck, his tongue moving down to my chest, squeezing my buttonholes with his teeth. It was a game we played often to see if we could undress each other without using hands. Feet were allowed. I was more flexible than Jacob and with my foot could raise his jeans at the waist then lean over and unzip him with my front teeth. Too eager to be together, we rarely finished the game. That night, Jacob stopped after the first button and looked me straight in the eyes. "I lied."

"What?" I whispered.

"I lied," he said again.

"About what?"

"Sleeping with Leann."

"When?"

"After our senior party."

He sounded like a voice from the basement, not Jacob, some weasel in a soap opera, doing what weasels do: wave their prick. I stared back, confused. "Leann? Why?"

"Too much liquor, hormones on overdrive. I drove back to her house after I took you home."

"Why tell me now?"

He didn't say a word, just rested his head on my bosom. What could I do? Leann was the past, and Jacob, a drunk teenage boy. I didn't ask questions, just lay there with him against me. We fell asleep before the coals turned into glowing embers.

"What?" she asked sensing my attention.

"I've never seen you in the daylight," I said.

"And?"

"You're just as beautiful."

She laughed and added, "Come on professor. You can do better than that."

"I'm in a diminished capacity."

—Jacob Hall, "Behold, I Give You the Power"

# Chapter 7

Trion, Alabama
Saturday, September 14, 2019
9:45 a.m.

Mike puts the drugs in the console. "Where to?"

"Heavenly Baked Goods and La Conchita." Heavenly is on Rose Road, two blocks through the traffic light and near Mt. Calvary Baptist Church with its neon *Jesus Is Coming Soon* sign. The road used to be called Polecat until the residents got fed up with being referred to as skunks and petitioned the City Council to change the name to Rose.

Aunt Grace and I went to Heavenly almost every Saturday morning, but not before I read her a chapter from one of the books she'd brought from the library. It all started with *Alice in Wonderland*. We'd sit at the kitchen table so she could drink her coffee while I ran my finger under the words and articulated each one like a lesson in elocution. Then she'd take me to buy a dozen brown butter chocolate chip cookies. I can still smell their sweet and nutty aroma and feel my aunt's shoulder, my pillar when she'd lift me up to look in the kitchen and watch Mrs. Cross at the oven. She pulled out a pan of the loveliest cookies I'd ever seen.

Mrs. Cross's granddaughter, now Heavenly's owner, fills the boxes with the four dozen cookies Susan has ordered. "These are in memory of Doctor Hall," she says, giving them to me.

When I get back in the truck, Mike breaks into his big smile. "I'd forgotten what they smell like," he says and grabs a cookie.

"Why don't you say please?" I tap Mike on the wrist before placing the cookies on the back bench seat.

"I don't know if I can make it to Susan's without another one."

"We also need to stop at La Conchita."

"What are you getting there?" he asks.

"*Tres leches* cake."

"A what?"

"Sponge cake soaked in milk—sweetened condensed milk, evaporated milk, and half-and-half. Our Spanish Lit professor at USC always brought one to department parties. Jacob and I loved it. He called it cake ice cream, and I started making it on our birthdays."

"I thought you waited tables," Mike says. "Didn't know you cooked too."

"What about my brownies and fudge on Mother's black and white linoleum? Sticky as all get-out."

"You've always been messy."

When we pull up to La Conchita, he takes out his phone while I go inside. The owner and baker, Clara Garza, arranges sweet bread behind the glass: *beso, concha, cuerno, empanada, and oreja.* I love the apple empanadas like the half-moon fried pies Aunt Grace used to make, filling the dough with sliced Granny Smith apples and brown sugar before pinching together the edges and browning them in what she called her "fancy fry" skillet. Clara knows empanadas are my favorite and gives me one right from the oven.

"You're out early," she says, wiping her hands on her apron.

"My brother's driving, and he's up with the sun."

"Why doesn't he come in?"

I get Mike's attention and wave him in. Wearing the brave face of someone entering a doctor's office, he tries not to appear hyper aware.

"I want you to meet Clara. She's my pal from spin class."

Mike smiles, showing a mouth full of well-treated teeth, greeting everybody like a new customer. That's how he more than doubled the bank clientele after becoming manager.

"I've heard nice things about you," he says.

"Likewise," Clara says, shaking his hand. "Excuse the flour." With long black hair, streaked silver, she wears it in a lady bun at work.

"Did you make all these?" he asks, scanning the goods behind glass.

"A lot of it. I have other bakers to help."

Two young women with trays of elephant ears and more empanadas start arranging them on the counter. Recognizing Monique and Amada, my students from Trion CC, I leave Mike with Clara in conversation.

"Sorry to hear about Doctor Hall," Monique says, holding her tray while Amada lays out the empanadas, snug against each other, like a fan, their edges neatly pressed with a fork to seal the dough.

"It was a real shock," I say, wiping my mouth.

"I enjoyed hearing him talk about being a writer when he visited our English class," Monique says.

"Then he read that amazing story about the church fight," Amada adds.

"'The Incident at the First Baptist Church,'" I say, thinking about all the edits I made on that story. Even after publishing it in *The Southern Review*, Jacob always doubted whether he described the congregation's conflict with enough gravitas to show how the narrator was moved by their faith.

"Doctor Hall is one of the reasons I switched my major to English," Amada said.

"What are the others?" I ask.

"You," Amada says, blushing. "I'm going to be a writer," she adds as if there were no other choice.

"You *are* a writer," I say, recalling her written response to Jacob's presentation. I know that converted feeling. How Jacob can—no, could—change a person's life with the strength of his words. That's the way I felt years ago, the way Amada feels today. Words were his superpower for almost everyone in his trajectory. If only he could have believed in them.

I look up to see Clara emerging through the kitchen's swinging doors and carrying a cake box.

"I found some fresh berries for the top of the *tres leches*." She lifts the lid for a last peek before handing it to me. Covered in whipped cream with button raspberries radiating from the center, the cake looks divine. I want to swipe a fingerful.

"It's absolutely beautiful. He would love it."

She smiles and asks, "How did you sleep?"

"Fitfully. Visiting hours drained me."

She moves closer and places her hand on mine. "You'll miss him forever," she says. "With time, you'll learn to live with this awful feeling."

"He took part of me with him."

Clara rubs my arm. "He left part of himself here with you. Do you want a ride to the funeral?"

"Cindy's going to pick me up."

Leaning against his truck, Mike finishes a *concha* and cleans his hands with a napkin before opening the door for me.

"You ready?" he asks.

"Let's go to Susan's," I say, waving to Clara.

He pulls out of the drive and I stare out the window at the sun breaking through clouds.

"That's the first time I've been there."

"Clara's quite the baker," I say, balancing the cake on my lap.

"That cookie—"

"*Concha*," I interrupt.

"—is tasty. I could have eaten two."

"Why didn't you buy some?"

"With those cookies, Leann's sandwiches, and the food Mary Jane's taking, I don't think we need them."

"We never need sweets. They taste good. And this is the time to spoil ourselves," I say.

"For sixty-six years I've been spoiling myself. Mary Jane says if I don't stop, I'll wind up in the funeral home. I point out that I'm going there no matter what."

"What happened to 'fit as a fiddle'?"

"That's my opinion." He smiles.

"You used to stay slim without much trouble."

"Until I quit smoking. Pounds are harder to keep off now."

"What about your treadmill?"

"I never use it. Plop in front of NCIS and eat M&Ms."

He's eaten plain M&Ms for as long as I remember. Every Christmas I order him two pounds in their original colors: red, yellow, tan, green, and brown.

The ten-minute drive to Susan's takes me past the high school, a landmark before I was born. Trion High is in the same three-story, red brick building where my mother and my mother's mother attended school. Two white columns stand on each side of the front doors, and the rooms are large with high ceilings. No air conditioning was installed until years after I graduated. With metal lockers lining the halls, they were always hot.

Even when Jacob and I were a couple, I felt like an outsider. I liked learning, liked reading, and hated that looks, popularity, and sucking up to the in-crowd were all that seemed to matter. I've never been to a reunion and never want to go, although Jacob went to a couple of his early ones, none in recent years. He tried to coax me into going with him. I refused.

As a kid, I felt trapped here, and Jacob became my way out—the beginning of a life filled with hope and ideas, the vision of a new day. He said small towns are for the small-minded. And I agreed. But I've begun to realize that my world is like a worn Samsonite suitcase I carry wherever I go, scratched and dented with locks that can pop open at any time.

She laughed again as she turned her black Ford F-150 into a crowded, gravel parking lot in front of a single-story, red-brick building. A white cross was painted on the wall to the left of the door. A small sign that read Red Rock Holiness Church was posted on the door.

—Jacob Hall, "Behold, I Give You the Power"

# Chapter 8

The Smith House
Saturday, September 14, 2019
10:15 a.m.

Mike turns into Susan's drive, which is defined by two brick walls. Her husband Larry has dental offices in Trion, Lakeport, and Boaz. His TV ads feature a bevy of young blonde girls with wide smiles and perfect teeth. A billboard on Highway 431 pictures his daughter, Crystal, smiling above the slogan *Straight and White Are What We Deliver*, which could have been the motto of Trion High.

Susan, Larry, and Crystal live in Country Club Estates across 431 in the same development where Mike lives. Their house is a huge one-story pink brick that they've expanded. First, they added a bedroom suite with a walk-in closet and shower/bath/jacuzzi for Crystal. Then they turned part of the original two-car garage into an elaborate TV room and built a separate three-car garage with an upstairs for a tanning bed and workout equipment plus a bathroom and shower.

About five years ago, Jacob and I used that shower together when he visited Susan and I visited Aunt Grace.

"How much did this palace cost?" I ask.

"No telling," Mike says, turning off the engine.

Like the golf course, the front yard is vibrant green, with sprinklers going off every twenty-four hours. Dwarf boxwood shrubs hold the grass like a fence. On the front stoop are two white Greek urns scrolled around the top and filled with red geraniums. Susan hires Pack's Garden Center to change the flowers according to the season. Red and white poinsettias for December, yellow daffodils for April, and pink azaleas for the summer. While not a gardener herself, she wants to exhibit her lawn and house. I once told Jacob they tried to keep up with the Joneses. He said they were the Joneses.

In a lavender silk robe, with lavender rollers in her hair, Susan meets us at the door. Typical of many well-to-do Trion wives in their early sixties, she puts on makeup first thing in the morning. Lots of black smudged eyeliner to emphasize her fairly large brown eyes. Jacob called them "bug eyes" because they dominate her round face. I think they're lovely—a dark depth with a kind of amber glow in the right light. Through the years, Susan has collected extra weight, giving her a more motherly look no matter what she wears, jeans or some expensive pants suit. Yet her brown eyes are still stunners. Her husband's standing comment is, "I'll never make your brown eyes blue." They're big country music fans, too, and Susan especially likes Loretta Lynn and her sister Crystal Gayle.

"Come in. I'm having a Bloody Mary."

We follow her to the kitchen, a *Southern Living* showcase. It has wood floors with a cotton-wool runner, stainless steel appliances, cabinets with glass panels so her Wedgewood china is on full display, and a kitchen table with an oval oak top. Mike places the cookies on the counter, and Susan slides the sandwiches into a stuffed fridge.

"The cake needs to be refrigerated, too," I say, handing it to Susan.

"What is this?" she asks, opening the box.

"*Tres leches* cake."

"No room in this fridge," she says. "Be a sweetheart and take it out to the garage."

Feeling dismissed, as often I do with her, I follow instructions. When I switch on the garage light, the neat and well-organized room amazes me. Pine shelves flank the beige drywalls and hold stacks of clear plastic containers with everything from folded baby clothes and a dismantled toy train to jeans Susan and Larry probably outgrew decades ago. They keep the past within immediate reach, maybe the only trait Susan shared with Jacob.

Susan and Larry's old fridge, now home to spillovers, is packed with trays of cheese and crudités, one on top of the other. Among the cheddar and carrots, I manage to eke out some space. A red lawn sign that reads ROY MOORE in bold caps leans against the wall. It's depressing how similar Susan's garage is to Mike's. I tear up. They both have daughters. After turning off the light, I dry my eyes and walk back to the kitchen.

Susan holds a pitcher of Bloody Marys.

"Want one?" she asks, reaching for the glasses.

I add two celeries and extra onions to mine.

We sit at the kitchen table, looking out on the ninth hole of the Trion Country Club Golf Course, its fairway watered and manicured like Susan's yard.

"I'm sorry for your loss," Mike says after a long swallow. "Ken, Paul, Charlie, and I gave Jacob a tribute at last night's game."

"Larry told me about it," Susan says. "He said y'all did a great job."

"We all loved him. He was a great guy," Mike says.

"He was a great brother. Always watched out for me as a little girl."

"You never needed watching out for," Mike says.

"You know what I mean. Kept the hungry boys away."

"I haven't heard that expression in a while," I say, biting the end of my celery.

"You'll be glad to know you'll be the only ex-wife there. Nora can't make it. The girls are coming, of course," Susan says and hands us the program for the church service.

"How are they?"

"Not sure. Crying, Jane called early this morning and said she talked to her dad the night before he died. She thought he sounded down, but no more than usual when talking about a new story where he couldn't settle on the ending. I didn't speak to Ruth. She's more like their mother. Not a crier. Wants to look in control. Like you after the split," Susan says.

I take a gulp and read the program. Mike watches the golfers. I'm not surprised that only women are scheduled to speak at Jacob's service. He was a man equally comfortable with all genders, though he preferred female company in his later years.

"The girls are flying Delta nonstop from New York to Birmingham and catching the ten a.m. shuttle bus to Trion. We asked them to spend a couple of nights, but they said they had to get back to school."

"Is Crystal friendly with them?" I ask.

"They've never met," Susan says. "We've invited them down, and they've never come. I get the feeling they think we're country. You understand that attitude, don't you, Janet?"

Bitch.

"How is Crystal? I haven't seen her on campus."

"I don't know if I like her taking college classes," Susan says. "She's a high school senior. Did you know she cut her hair short like Kristen Stewart's?"

"Less to do in the morning," I answer.

"Makes her look like a … Yankee," Susan says.

I open the program and notice that Crystal will speak.

"What's she going to say at the service?" I ask.

"She'll read from one of Jacob's stories."

"Which one?"

"She won't tell me."

"I'm sure she'll choose a good passage. Crystal's always been smart," I say. "Maybe she'll connect with her cousins."

"The twins never have cared for anything that has to do with their dad."

"Where's Larry?" I ask.

"At the office. Dalia Gray rang at seven a.m. She hasn't slept a wink because her daughter's braces are hurting so bad."

Mike continues to watch the golfers.

"Susan, do you know if Jacob had a history of heart problems?"

"Never talked about his health. Like Dad, Jacob always said he was fine."

"He'd say the same to me. Hardly ever went to a doctor."

A golf ball bounces into Susan's yard.

"Do they ever come in and get their balls?" Mike asks. Now we all watch the golfer drop another ball, hit it, and drive off.

"No. Our Pomeranian, Lucy, raises holy hell if they do."

"What do you do with all those balls?" Mike asks.

"Larry collects them in a trash can in the garage. Want some?"

"Sure. I play Pro Vs."

"Here's a bag," she says. "Go take what you want."

She turns to me. "What are you going to say at the service?"

"Not sure. What about you?"

"Talk about how much he loved it here and what a sweet brother he was."

Susan likes to think Jacob loved Trion so I don't say a word. I hear scratching at the back door, heavy nails tapping hard. "Is your Pomeranian on steroids?"

"Heavens, no," says Susan as she opens the door. "I brought home Willy, Jacob's Golden Lab." He bounds into the kitchen, soft ears flapping, paws reaching for our laps, with Lucy right behind. A prissy, cream-colored mess, the Pom has the run of the house, barking at everyone to be sure she gets full attention. Susan shakes some dry food into two bowls and the dogs start eating.

"You going to keep him?" I ask.

"He's not mine," she says.

"What do you mean?"

"Jacob left him to you."

"What!"

"Yep. The lawyer read me the will, and you're the proud mother."

"Jacob knew I didn't want a dog," I say.

"Well, you've got one now. We put too much money into this house to let the dogs take over. I don't want him near my fancy rugs and needlepoint chairs," she says as she closes all the kitchen doors.

Finished eating, Willy comes over and sits next to me, looking up with his brown eyes. I rub his head, feeling those short hairs tickle my palm, his tail pounding the floor. A large, exuberant dog, Willy is going to be a handful, more for me than for Rhoda. She'll just claw and hiss and leave him in a frenzy for me to take care of.

"I have a cat."

As usual, Susan ignores me and says, "Willy would destroy our house. Lucy's small and well trained. He's just too big for us."

"If Willy and Rhoda get along, no problem. It seems odd Jacob already had a will. Never been a planner except for his writing."

"About three months ago, he mentioned he was going to get a will. Wanted to be sure the girls got his house," Susan says. "Then he laughed that royalties could be an issue."

"He liked to imagine that his novel and handful of stories might be discovered someday, like Emily Dickinson's poetry," I say.

Mike comes back with a bag of balls. "Whose dog is that?" he asks Susan.

"He's going home with Janet."

"Not in my truck."

"Don't be so grumpy, Mike. My house is five minutes away. Anyway, if there's an accident, I'll clean it up."

"You don't even clean your own house, much less your car."

"Don't argue, siblings. Here're the food, his leash, and some treats. Need a bloody for the road?"

"Better not," I say.

"I'll give Willy a ride," Mike says, "but he has to travel in the bed."

After our goodbyes, Willy and I climb into the back of the truck and feel the wind on our faces. It's been a long time since I sat in the bed. I wish it were then—a summer night when I was young with a beer in my hand and gazing at the stars. Lightning bugs competed for attention. Life lay in front of us, and we thought we could fix any errors along the way.

Sitting beside me now, Willy enjoys the ride. Petting his head, I think about his instinctual life, unburdened by hope and memory. Existing in the moment and nothing more.

"Why are we here?"

"My Uncle John is preaching today. I'm not missing him for you."

With my best professorial stare, I radiated disapproval and disappointment, but what works on my freshmen didn't work on Georgia.

"You can wait out here or walk back to the County Line or come to the service," she said exiting her truck. "Want me to roll down the windows?"

—Jacob Hall, "Behold, I Give You the Power"

# Chapter 9

The Williams House
Saturday, September 14, 2019
11:30 a.m.

When I open my front door, Rhoda sees Willy and scrams to the bedroom. Jacob's dog stands there wagging his tail.

"Stay." And Willy stops tugging. "Sit." And, surprisingly, Willy sits. "Why are you here?" I ask, leading him to the kitchen and closing the kitchen door behind me.

He's a lovable Lab, as most are, rubbing against my leg and turning those big brown eyes up at me.

"Okay, boy." I unfasten the leash and hang it on the chair. Taking down two soup bowls, I fill one with water and shake Kibbles 'n Bits into the other. He's thirsty, sounding like a kid splashing in a tub as he laps water over his tongue onto the floor. While I sit in the chair and take off my Nikes, he gobbles the pellets.

"Wish you could talk." After dancing around the food, he lays his head on my lap. I run my fingers around his ears and down his back. He feels like somebody I've known all his life. Why did Jacob leave him to me? He knew I'm a cat person. He knew I didn't want a canine licking my toes and sticking to my side. A clinging pet, not remote and mysterious like a cat, who can use her litter box and cover her waste whereas a dog has to be walked and picked up after several times a day. Maybe that's exactly why you're here—Jacob still leaves the caretaking to me. Why didn't he tell me he had a will?

As if agreeing, as if I were his whole world now, including that fussy little feline, Willy looks again at me. Jacob was up to something. When he first adopted you, he sent a selfie. Jacob was in bed with his left arm draped over a skinny little puppy four months old that he found at the Rescue Center. He said you came to him immediately, licked his fingers through the cage bars. No hesitation. You had your shots and were ready for a soft bed and good food. From then on, you filled the empty place beside him. That was two years ago, about the time I left Columbia and moved back to Trion. Jacob said he rarely went anywhere without you.

I slide on my flip-flops to take Willy outside. Enclosing the backyard is a low cedar fence Aunt Grace installed. Not that she didn't like the neighbors. They were fine. She just didn't want them or their kids or their other animals taking shortcuts through her yard, exposing her to their gossipy eyes. I feel the same way. As soon as I open the back door, Willy jumps up and heads out, digging in the grass before I settle on the lawn chair, an old-fashioned type: aluminum, lightweight, blue-webbed chair that's sturdy, comfortable, and easy to move, probably a hit with hipsters. Willy at work takes inventory of the scents and begins to uproot the yard.

In a green plaid shirt and floppy straw hat, my neighbor, Miss Irene, who taught Jacob and me senior English, tends her roses, cutting deadheads and tossing them in a pile. Her garden abounds with what Aunt Grace called cotton roses, perennials that come back every spring. The round flower buds look like cotton bolls, and the leaves resemble hearts with pointed lobes like cotton foliage. Showy blooms about four inches across, the flowers blossom white in the fall, fade to pink as they age, and finally end up red before the winter freeze. Often all three colors appear on the same multi-trunked shrub five feet tall.

Miss Irene is my kind of gardener. She loves her backyard roses and front-yard azaleas, making sure all are carefully tended. Her ex-student Philip does the heavy work: fertilizing, watering, mulching, and cutting the grass. He's usually there on Saturday mornings to maintain *the grounds*—what she calls her half acre. Almost six feet tall with high cheekbones and sparkling blue eyes, she's the ideal neighbor, friendly enough to let me know she cares and reclusive enough to respect the space between.

Today when I wave, she moseys up to the fence.

"Sorry to hear about Jacob," she says, raising her husky voice just loud enough for me to hear.

"It was a shock."

"He was one of my favorite students. He asked questions, stayed after class, and wrote thoughtful essays. He wanted to learn." She adds, "You were smart and diligent, too, yet never as intense."

Miss Irene's senior English class was demanding. Jacob always read and edited my essays before I turned them in.

"What time's the service?"

"Two thirty."

"May I come over for a few minutes now? I have something for you."

Willy and I go back into the house. We're not there long when the doorbell rings. He barks but quietens when I say, "Hush." Miss Irene hands me a square Pyrex of mac and cheese covered in plastic wrap.

"My comfort food," I say, carrying it into the kitchen. "Thanks so much."

Petting Willy, she warns, "We'll get along just fine if you don't dig up my yard."

He wags his tail.

"Do you want something to drink?" I ask.

"No. You don't have a lot of time before the funeral."

"Sit down for a few minutes," I say, pouring myself some water and pulling out the saltines and Jiffy peanut butter.

"Think I will have a peanut butter cracker," she says, spreading the saltine. "Do you have a Coke? I'm glad you didn't change Grace's colors. I love turquoise and yellow."

"Mike wanted me to repaint so I could put it on the market."

"I helped Grace pick out these colors. Talking and drinking coffee, we spent a lot of time around this table."

"May I ask you something?"

"Shoot."

"Was Jacob a confident student?"

"Yes and no. Always wanted his work perfect."

*Even then*, I think.

"When I handed back final essays on 'The Raven,' he looked at his paper, then at me, glaring. The figure of speech about daggers comes to mind. I shall never forget how uneasy I felt."

"What did he say?"

"Nothing at first. I finished turning back papers, and students left for their next class. All except Jacob. He'd read a page then look at me before reading the next. It was the only time I saw his face turn bright red. He appeared at war with himself, conflicted between anger and sadness. When every other student was gone, he asked, 'Why did I make an eighty-six?'"

"Because you left out some of the key issues about rhyme and rhythm."

"'I analyzed how the lover was losing his mind over the death of Lenore, how the imagery got bleaker and bleaker.' I remember that exchange with him like it was yesterday. He was the rare student who actually loved literature and what I taught." Miss Irene sips her Coke. "You loved lit, too, Janet. It's why we ended up reading for a living. Jacob loved reading, but I always thought he was competing with the authors he read, wanted to beat them at their own game."

"He loved everything about the word," I say, hearing her own love for language.

"He seemed hard on himself. Never content with what he'd done," she says.

"The more he wrote, the less he submitted," I add. "Because it wasn't 'quite right.'"

"I read a few of his short stories. They are perfectly written. Each sentence …."

"That's the problem," I say. "Language over story."

"Why didn't you go for a doctorate?" Miss Irene asks.

"When we split, I needed money and was worn down by academics. By the time I felt like returning, I had too many papers to grade and too little time."

She looks at me pensively, as she did when I was her student, then says, "Maybe you're meant to be a great teacher."

We sit quietly. Finally, she says, "I won't be at the funeral. The older I get, the more people I lose. Each loss is harder to bear. Especially Jacob. He was too young to leave. He had so much more to give."

Miss Irene swipes one more cracker with peanut butter before standing. "Mind if I take a look at Grace's study on the way out?"

"Not at all. It's just as she left it. I think of that room as my aunt personified."

We walk to the study. Miss Irene steps over the threshold and stops, scanning everything there like recording the view for later reflection. A blonde oak desk faces west beneath a picture window that looks onto the side yard full of azalea bushes of rainbow colors: white, orange, pink, and red. Pictures of Aunt Grace line the window ledge: Aunt Grace with Farah Fawcett bangs, Aunt Grace with a pixie cut and black jeans, Aunt Grace in a McGovern T-shirt. Then two pictures of her with Miss Irene. In both, they're holding hands. I hear Miss Irene clear her throat, reminding me how much she cried at the funeral.

"Saying goodbye is mighty painful," she says. After a few minutes, we walk outside. Willy follows. She pauses in the drive. "I wish I'd given him a better grade on that essay. I was harder on him than on the other students. He had so much talent. I wanted to push him. We all did what we thought best. The road of regret often is paved with good intentions that cause a world of suffering. Please forgive my sentimentality. It's close at hand more and more these days."

She walks back to her house. I wait on the stoop as Mother taught me—watch people leave until they're safely out of sight. Once I asked her why. "You never know when it's the last time you'll see them." I thought her behavior reflected her country ways. Now I understand.

I'm surprised I can hold in my tears. Maybe my body knows they'll be needed later.

My cell phone dead, the next twenty minutes were spent leaning
against Georgia's truck, vaping and analyzing the cultural
implications of the assembled vehicles. Most were domestic. Red was a
popular color, attributed to either political or sport affiliation, and I
wondered what color they would have chosen if the Crimson Tide had
been the Blue Wave. The absence of orange cars was most likely self-
selection. Auburn fans have their own country church. This rural
church was nothing like churches at home in a midwestern city where
they have steeples, stained glass windows, paved parking lots, and
carefully tended grass. Our God wanted us to see an oasis not a VFW
hall in decline.

—Jacob Hall, "Behold, I Give You the Power"

# Chapter 10

The Williams House
Saturday, September 14, 2019
12:15 p.m.

"Let's go in, Willy," I say as my phone lights up with a text from
Cindy: `I'll pick you up at 1:30`. When I open the door to the
hall, Rhoda's waiting. Willy bounces up to her, and she hisses one of
those long get-the-fuck-out-of-my-house hisses. He stops, and she
scratches him hard. Willy's the one who runs this time, slouching under
the table. Taunting him, Rhoda sits in the doorway.

"Kids. This is not going to be easy. You've got to endure each other.
Or one of you will wind up in a place where the food and company are
not so appealing." Closing the door behind us, I pet Willy and join
Rhoda. "Okay, Rhoda. You're the adult here. Leave Willy alone. If he
wants to play, just do what you usually do to me. Ignore him and leave."
I reach down and rub in front of her ears.

Retrieving the funeral program from my shoulder bag, I see my
name first among those to speak. I've written nothing. A feeling of
betrayal consumes me every time I open the laptop or pick up a pen.
The eulogy will finish Jacob. I can't imagine living in this world without
him. Though married only ten years and divorced more than thirty-five,
we've never really been disconnected since we were teenagers.

What to say at Jacob's service? For whom is a funeral? The living or the dead? If the living, what do they want to hear about the dead when they were alive? Like the truth about most of us, the full truth about Jacob lies in what we don't want to hear. He was what my mother would call a *womanizer*, not the most flattering of words. I knew he enjoyed the company of women. In many ways he brought out their best. What they read, the music they liked, what their dreams were, how marriage figured into their lives. Essentially, he listened to them, their ups, their downs. What it was like at home, their relationship with their kids, their husband.

Until Jacob told me about Leann, I didn't suspect him. I didn't know he was such a good liar. I always knew that women wanted to fuck him, and I took some pleasure in their visible desire, watching them flirt with him and he with them. Because he was mine, I endured it. Yet after his confession, I began to wonder. Early on I was trusting and thought—or wanted to think—that Jacob, while he cherished my mind and heart, also cherished my body. And he did. But I thought he loved it as I did his. That we were a monogamous pair. I'd never been with anyone else.

After opening my eyes to a world wider than a girl's snow globe, I realized that he never curbed his sexual appetite. Another girl here or there was just a side dish, though he didn't confess to any transgressions beyond Leann. Was my urge to find myself really my desire to be away from his scattered sex life? If I wasn't his wife, I had no investment in what he did or didn't do with his penis. My key concern was that if we continued to have sex, I wanted it clean. I didn't want herpes or crabs or any other sexual sickness that a wanton penis brought. Jacob understood.

His heart belonged to me, or so I thought until he met Nora. She was still an ingenue, looking up to Jacob with an admiring twinkle the way we all did when we were first around him. And I began to feel a growing distance between Jacob and me. He didn't talk about her much, but when he did, I felt a softness in his voice. He was smitten. He was at that age where he wanted progeny. When we married, we'd agreed that enough people already existed in the world and we had no need to crowd the space with our offspring. What were kids anyway if not parents' selfish desire to sow their genes? We had each other and books and writing and teaching. Further along in our marriage, those were no longer enough for Jacob. He wanted to plant his DNA. He began to talk about children, and I'd cut him off with "You know I don't want them. I thought we'd settled that." He brought the subject up less and less frequently after meeting Nora.

One year after our divorce, he married her and stayed married just long enough to beget the twins, Ruth and Jane. They were all he had in common with his second wife. He called me to complain about Nora's demands: prodding him to make more money, to leave teaching and become an administrator. She tore down his pages and once burned them in the fireplace when he was teaching, saying their house was not a public laundry. "The sex isn't all that good either," he said. Over the years, the late night and early morning calls became regular, especially after she was gone. When I moved back to Trion, calls came almost every night. Sometimes an hour long, sometimes longer, depending on when we had to get up.

At Jacob's service, the community doesn't want to hear about his complexities, reflective of our own complexly ambivalent lives. No, those folks who come to Jacob's farewell want to hear about his esteemed qualities, how he helped shape an improved existence. And that's what I'll tell them. How Jacob led me to a place where I could find my better self, spread my wings and fly. They want me to praise Caesar. And I will.

I force myself to walk to the study and start jotting down the kind things about Jacob that I love, always have. Maybe I should read something he's written, part of a story or one of his poems. He was shy about his writing, never sure he'd done it right, always trying to fly higher. He said Faulkner had done it, taken the holy word and put it in the mouths of every character he created so their tongues became vessels of truth, catching the mean and sweet in all of us. I reach for *As I Lay Dying*, dog-eared with no cover, moved from shelf to shelf, Alabama to South Carolina and back. The first book Jacob ever gave me. It talks about how living prepares us for dying. Now when the time's here and I must look death head on, I'm afraid. Without Jacob, what happens to me? Why couldn't I have been the first to leave this body like a tenant moving to a new country?

The doorbell rings, breaking my reverie. I don't want to answer it. If I don't, I won't have to go to the church and I won't have to talk about Jacob and if I don't talk about him, they can't bury him and if they can't bury him, he won't really be dead. All I have to do is sit here and ignore the fucking doorbell. Yet Willy begins barking. He lets me know Jacob has to stay dead, and I have to let in Cindy.

"Why aren't you dressed?" she asks. "And what's with the dog?" Seven months ago she returned to Trion for the same reason I'd returned: her parents left her their home. She retired from being a props manager at an Atlanta film company.

"This is Willy. Jacob left him to me in the will," I explain as he runs toward me.

"That Jacob, always the final word," she says.

"Maybe he meant well."

"Why do you apologize for him?"

"Maybe he wanted someone to watch over me."

"Yeah, right. A canine caretaker."

"Seriously. Maybe Jacob wanted me to have a part of him."

"So he leaves you his needy Lab."

"Don't be flippant," I say on my way to the bedroom to dress.

"When are you going to stop making excuses for him?"

"I did when we divorced."

"You're like a mother who's stingy with praise to keep her kid from getting a swollen head, but Lord save the fool who criticizes her baby," Cindy says. "I'm getting a beer. Why would Jacob put the dog in the will?" she asks, petting Willy. "Is Rhoda in your will?"

"I don't have a will."

"Was Jacob sick?"

"Not that I know. Susan doesn't know either. Take Willy out to pee." Not hearing a yes, I stick my head outside the bedroom door and add a "Please." Cindy shepherds him out.

My black pants suit with the white lace bib looks good with my two-inch pumps. I pull my hair back into a chignon with the black Japanese chopsticks, inlaid with pearl, that Jacob gave me on our first anniversary. I wrap my hair around the sticks a few times before pushing the skinny ends into the back of the wrap. He liked my hair up, and I often liked pleasing him. Superstitious about funerals, I usually wear something to the service that connects me to the deceased. For Aunt Grace, I wore my peace necklace.

Closing the bedroom door for Rhoda's solitude, I leave with Cindy. Her driving's a little jerky for my taste, but this is not a day I want to be behind the wheel. Not sure I trust myself.

"I saw Leann this morning."

"That cow!"

"She muttered something about good times with Jacob."

"Once a cow, always a cow."

"Jacob fessed up."

"Every time they fucked?"

"Do you know something I don't? He said it only happened once," I say, knowing she's right but damn if I'm going to admit it.

She takes a quick turn on Dunn Street.

"What are you going to say at the service?" Cindy asks.

"I have no fucking clue."

The faint sound of voices and a keyboard could be heard, and I discerned or imagined a few "Amens." The volume rose as a guitar joined the keyboard. The music was spirited and more competent than expected.

—Jacob Hall, "Behold, I Give You the Power"

# Chapter 11

Second Methodist Church
Saturday, September 14, 2019
1:45 p.m.

Cindy pulls her Honda into the church parking lot, already full of trucks and SUVs, mostly Ford and GM. Crimson Tide red is the most popular color. Truth be known, the First Methodist disbanded in the mid-70s when the preacher and several church stewards were caught wife swapping. The congregants splintered with some becoming Baptists, a few joining the snake-handling group on the mountain outside Trion, and the rest taking up golf and sleeping in. Mother always said, "Thank God for Calvary Baptist."

"There's a pack of Marlboro Reds in the glove compartment. Would you hand them to me, please," Cindy says.

After we get out of the car, we stay in the parking lot for her to have a smoke.

"I thought you quit."

"Weddings and funerals don't count," she answers, flipping back the cardboard top. She lifts a cigarette with her teeth and lights it with a click of her green Bic, inhaling deeply like the intake was her last. I resist noting that the Bic came from Cindy's purse and watch her blow the smoke upward in a spiral that rolls through the air and disappears. There's pleasure in that first drag after hours of abstinence.

"Do you miss smoking?" she asks.

"At first a lot, not so much now."

"Do you want one?" she asks with an impish grin like offering me a line of coke.

"Took twenty pounds, countless bags of hard candy, and a lot of cavities to kick the habit ten years ago," I say, still following the smoke.

"Didn't touch the deadly sticks 'til my freshman year in college," she says. "Then I took drag after drag, coughing alone in my dorm room, learning how to look like a pro." After the next draw, she opens her mouth and pushes out the smoke with her tongue while inhaling it though her nose.

"I thought French inhaling was cool and sexy until my sinuses began to feel like shit. The guys loved it," she says.

"Jacob had a real smoking fetish. He liked to watch me bring a slim, long cigarette to my lips then perform what he called the 'oral act' of inhaling and exhaling. When I finished the cigarette, he was ready to fuck. Always put a pack of Virginia Slims in my Christmas stocking."

"What made you quit?"

"Aunt Grace's emphysema. She gasped for air while lighting another."

"I'm like a chipper now," Cindy says.

"A chipper?"

"Someone who can do heroin just on the weekends. Cigs don't have their claws in me anymore."

She drops the butt on the pavement and rubs it out with the sole of her shoe. I look down. She sighs, picks it up, field dresses it, and drops the filter back in the pack. We gaze at the mourners outside the church. The women and men are segregated as they were at our first junior high dance. They are old. They are white. And I recognize almost everybody. The homogeneity is like our Trion classes in the late 60s and early 70s. Both Cindy and I left Trion for places more diverse and relatively liberal for the deep South.

"Looks like 1972 here," I say.

"My graduation," she adds. "They even dress the same. Mostly the guys."

"Do you miss Atlanta?"

"When I left Trion High for Georgia State, I was a little scared. Never been away from home for any length of time. Not even to summer camp. Atlanta was hopping. Drinking age eighteen. Nudie clubs everywhere. It was something to behold for a Southern Baptist girl from Sand Mountain. "And I'd go back in no time if I could take the house with me."

"I'm not sure the house is worth staying for anymore," I say.

"That's the grief talking. Come on, girl. Time to face old Trion." She takes my elbow.

As we head toward the church, Cindy intercepts a couple of high school friends. After last night, I try to avoid the crowd much as I still feel their eyes on me, their disdain for my divorcing Jacob. My pulse begins to race. All I want to do is sneak into the sanctuary and hide off to the side. Susan has instructed me to sit in the first couple of rows. I leave Cindy and see Ken handing out programs at the door. He gives me a quick hug, and I walk to the front and sit in the second pew. "Amazing Grace" floats through the air. The pianist is Marcella Jones, someone I grew up with, someone who knew Jacob, knew what a rebel he was when it came to Christian convention. Despite his dad being a steward and his mama teaching Sunday school, he refused to go to church after he was legal. In Trion being legal was being sixteen, when you could receive a state driver's license and take yourself anywhere you wanted to go.

Sunday mornings he'd pick me up in his red truck and drive miles through soybean and corn fields. Alabama used to be called "The Cotton State" when cotton was king in the nineteenth century, although much of the cotton land was abandoned by the late 1960s. Jacob and I would take the quilt, find a place near the Alabama River, and act as if we were in another world. My Baptist parents thought I was going with him to the Methodist Church.

Looking around the sanctuary, I notice not much has changed. There's a kneeling rail curved like a half moon with corduroy cushions the color of lapis lazuli in the front, separating the congregation from the minister and choir. The pulpit's centered behind the rail, the choir in a loft with a piano on either side, and a four-foot wooden cross behind the minister. Tragic Jesus with his red stigmata and blond curls was removed thirty years ago when an evangelical group called it idolatry.

The last church I stepped foot in was Calvary Baptist three years ago for Aunt Grace's funeral. Like Jacob's, her service was a closed casket. None of that crying and screaming over a dead body before it was lifted away. My aunt knew exactly what she wanted: peace lilies everywhere and a bouquet of them on her casket. Not a bed of white carnations or white roses. A full bouquet of peace lilies. She said Jesus was the lily of the field and that's all she needed for her own farewell. When her casket passed by, the sun shone through the stained glass and cast a blue tint on all the flowers.

I wonder what Jacob would say about this Christian display with its bed of red and white roses. His spirit probably flew away the moment he fell to the floor attacked by his heart, by me who disconnected him. I feel something press against my leg and look to the side to see Cindy, who just slid in. Taking her hand, I feel consoled that she's there.

The side door opens, and Jacob's twin girls are followed by Nora, a surprise since Susan said she wasn't coming. Mother and daughters sit directly in front of us in the first row. I know the first ex should acknowledge and maybe even comfort the second ex. There's a certain relief in thinking that Jacob's friends can direct some of their anger at Nora now. Still girly pretty as she was years ago, this is the first time

I've seen her since graduate school. She's wearing a black chiffon dress with cap sleeves, and has a long, brown ponytail. The twins look like almost every other southern girl these days. Skinny and blonde from the bottle. Except for their brilliant brown eyes, I can't see anything of Jacob. They are Nora's daughters.

I tap Nora's shoulder. "Susan wasn't sure you were coming."

"The girls said I should," she replies. They turn around.

"Dad told us about you," Ruth says.

"I hope it was good."

"Too good," Jane adds.

"Amazing Grace" fades into "Blessed Assurance," and people finish taking their seats. Susan, Larry, and Crystal sit beside Nora and the twins. Cindy squeezes my arm, and my heart beats even faster. My mouth is dry and sticky, and I want to run away and hide as the minister takes his place at the front. He's young, possibly forty, no noticeable gray, and wears a blue robe with a scarlet shawl. The church has become more formal over the years. The music dies down as he asks us to bow our heads. "Lord, we've come today to say goodbye to one of your blessed children who'll soon be home with you. We thank you for the time he spent among us as you graced us with his presence. Watch over us now while we say farewell to his spirit, hoping to join him one day on the other side. Yours in gratitude. Amen."

With those last words, I shiver, knowing my time is near. Clutching a piece of crumpled note paper on which I've written Jacob and drawn a heart around his name as I did in high school, I walk to the podium, fearing I'll trip on the way. To steady myself, I grip the sides of the cherry wood pulpit and look into a host of faces, many familiar, tilting up, mouths slightly open, some with anger, some with disdain, some I imagine thinking *but for the grace of God go I*, and most hungry for some piece of Jacob that they can carry forever.

"On our first date Jacob brought me flowers. I gave him my copy of *The Optimist's Daughter* by Eudora Welty. When I asked Jacob why he asked me out, he said because he saw my name in the library books he read. We were both readers. But Jacob was more than a reader. He was a writer. Being a writer, he wanted to unlock the truth of people, even if that truth was marred by sin and ugliness. Yet he always found beauty in the end. Despite our ups and downs, we never lost the bond we formed that first night.

"Jacob gave me one last gift. He left me his dog, a Golden Lab named Willy after William Faulkner, from whom my cat Rhoda hides. Jacob knew I'm a cat lady at heart." Amid waves of laughter, I pause, surprised by its suddenness.

"I guess he wanted to be sure I was taken care of, and we all know that Labradors are lovable caretakers. Though we divorced more than thirty-five years ago, we talked and wrote to each other, and during the last ten years we saw each other at conferences, in Illinois, and here in Trion. I want to honor the best friend I've ever had, the seventeen-year-old who showed me life within the pages of books, one page after another opening up worlds of beauty and adventure. A man who led me through college and graduate school. That's the boy, the man I loved all these years. Even after the divorce, he was always there for me. The friend I relied on when Aunt Grace died."

I look at the audience looking back at me, feel their arms extend with a warmth I've never felt before in Trion. I know Jacob is pleased. He hears something meant only for him, a kind of thankfulness I seldom expressed, that he rarely heard from me.

"Faulkner said, 'The past is never dead. It's not even past.' Jacob will always be with us. I should never have left him. He was my Samson." My voice cracks, and I try to breathe deeper to hold back tears. My words wake remorse that I've wrestled with but never made public, not even to Cindy. I glance at Nora, who's looking down. Cindy, her eyes wide, looks straight at me. The minister touches my elbow, and I turn. He hugs me before I walk back to the pew. Cindy puts her arms around me, reassuring me that I won't fall.

***

After the service is over, we exit by rows. Susan, Larry, and Crystal are followed out by Nora and the twins with Cindy and me behind. I imagine all the eyes of Trion fixed on me. Why in hell did I call Jacob my Samson? I swear Charlie is humming those Tom Jones lyrics: why, why, why Delilah.

When I step out of the church, the sun burns my eyes, and I shade them with my left hand, seeing Nora and the twins disappear into a black sedan. Susan's left already, Ken looks very solemn, Cindy walks off to smoke a cigarette, and Clara stands in the shade of a red maple. Since I didn't notice her in the sanctuary, I assume she sat in a back row because she was late or chose to keep to herself.

"Are you all right?" she asks.

"No, but I'll make it."

"You damn well better."

"Was my eulogy terrible?"

"The Samson reference surprised me," Clara replies.

"I don't know what came over me. I should have written out what to say."

The mourners move to their cars while Cindy leans against her

Honda, looking at her watch then at me.

"You never know what grief will utter," Clara says.

"Probably some kind of Freudian slip. Everybody thinks I betrayed their golden boy."

"Not everybody," she says and puts her arms around me. Detecting a faint trace of baked bread, I find her waist and take comfort in her being there.

A honk intrudes, and I know Cindy, for whom being late is a cardinal sin, will honk again.

"Thanks for coming, Clara."

"Remember, no one offered any silver coins, and you didn't cut away his power. Give yourself a break," Clara says. "See you at the cemetery."

After watching her reach her car, I join Cindy.

"What the hell," I told the empty parking lot and opened the door.
—Jacob Hall, "Behold, I Give You the Power"

# Chapter 12

Jackson Memorial Cemetery
Saturday, September 14, 2019
3:45 p.m.

It's warm on this tail end day of summer. The cemetery looks like one of the richest, manicured lawns in Trion with short blades of grass and lush leaves for this time of year. Plenty of summer rain has left the earth vibrant. Nonetheless, I feel more like one of the cemetery's stone maidens, the flow of tears dammed inside. I'm the last to take my seat, second row behind Susan and Larry and next to Nora. Her girls are in front with Crystal. The coffin rests on two straps above the open grave.

Standing on the other side of the casket, Reverend Warren begins. "Jacob, during our sorrow and loss, we thank you for living your life among us. We are grateful for your gentleness and compassion, your strength and endurance. We take joy in knowing that you're going to your eternal home. We ask you now for forgiveness for any hurt we may have given you, and we forgive you for any hurt you may have given us. You're released into the Everlasting Arms. May you know wholeness and peace now and through all eternity." With every word Larry and Susan nod. Crystal and the girls sit still.

When Jacob is lowered into the earth, something cracks inside me. I feel the end—the final time I'll be anywhere near his body even though I know he's already gone. The last we talked, when I said, "Either come back to Trion, or I'm done," I'd felt my own desperation. We'd outlived our dreams; two aging people whose futures receded into our pasts, who saw each other and remembered a time long lost when we were kids eager to escape the loss and sadness of our parents. We used to feel the land held us back. The very soil that grew us choked us. We left, young and fresh enough to believe, deeply believe, that our journey together would not be in vain.

Jacob came back. But he's the one who cut me off, and the entire world. Now he's planted in the red soil of Trion, buried beneath the weight of the past. All hope stuffed into a dark hole. Nothing left except pain and heartache. No eternal home. No everlasting arms.

Reverend Warren's voice breaks my nightmare. "There'll be a wake at Susan and Larry's, five to ten p.m. Please come by and continue to celebrate Jacob."

At the end of the reverend's invitation, the cemetery employees finish lowering the coffin, signifying that the services are over. Pulling two red roses from a standing urn, I drop them on his casket and blow a kiss. Nora and the girls leave with Susan and Larry, who walk to their car, Larry's arm around Susan's shoulder, Crystal following. Her short blonde hair with dark roots is at odds with her namesake's knee-length tresses. Pausing, Crystal looks back to offer me a small, open-palm wave that provides disproportionate comfort. In gratitude, I bring my palms to my heart and slightly bow to her, who smiles and turns away to join her parents in their enormous SUV.

Clara hugs me from behind. "I'm so sorry, Janet. I know how close you were."

"From our first date, he became my best friend in sickness and in health."

"He'll always be with you," she says, hugging me again.

"Are you going to the wake?"

"I don't think so. Groups of Trionites unnerve me. I'm not good with small talk."

"I totally get it," I say and hug her.

Mike walks over, and Clara leaves us by ourselves as she meanders through the tombstones.

"I'm going to go see Mama," he says.

"Good," I reply.

"Join me?"

"I'll stop by. I want to visit Aunt Grace's plot first."

"See you at Susan and Larry's," he says and gives me a bear hug. Over his shoulder, Mary Jane's busy on her phone.

Staring at Jacob's grave, I want to climb in, privately say good-bye, tell him I'm sorry, kiss him one last time. Even if I did climb in, I wouldn't be able to tell him untruths, not now, not today, when he's leaving for good. I meant what I said and now it's come true. A polite clearing of a throat startles me, and I turn to see Ken.

"The boys will be done in about two hours," he says. Beyond him are two cemetery workers by a truck.

"No hurry. I don't think I'll come back 'til tomorrow."

"Sorry about Jacob," Ken says and hugs me harder than before. "I like what you said about Jacob giving you his Golden Lab as a caretaker."

"I know he adored Willy. He was always sending me selfies."

"What's the saying? A man loves his dog more than he loves himself."

"Never heard that one. I'm going to visit Aunt Grace before leaving." I turn and walk away.

Patches of cut grass separate family lots marked by large granite or marble monuments, usually inscribed with the family name. Letters etched into stone, the crevices black with time, give the name a kind of bas relief. Trion churches still observe Decoration Sunday during the warm months of May and September, with each church specifying which Sunday. It's an occasion for families to come together, especially those from out of town. They arrive a day or two early to work at the plot. With hoes and shovels, they scrape the ground, make new plantings, and prune older ones. At the site, a Sunday picnic dinner with church singing follows cleanup.

Although I rarely go to church or celebrate Decoration Day, I check on Aunt Grace's plot to see how the azaleas are doing. Soon after moving back, I planted two snow azaleas there, knowing how much she loved those flowers. Leggy shrubs, they're nearly five feet tall and are covered in small white blooms that explode from the earth mid-April to early May. In August, I collect the floral remains and spread them under the bushes at home, imagining her spirit hovers somewhere close.

Visiting her usually lifts me. I need her during this despair. Why Jacob? Why did his heart betray him? He was only sixty-six years old and on the brink of starting over with me. He never showed any sign of heart problems that I know of. He drank too much bourbon and smoked too many cigarettes. Are they why he left so early? Or did I send him away? Were my words the tipping point? Did I push him into his grave? Please, Grace, speak to me. Let me hear you. What am I to do? Did I kill the person I loved most in this world?

My head hurts. Leaning against the magnolia tree, I hear a muffled horn and see Cindy's Honda, the only car in view. I kiss my palm and hold it hard against Aunt Grace's headstone.

Later, I would remember that the building could have been anything from a bar to a hardware store to a church. It was a rectangle, unencumbered by any other distinguishing feature. The oak cross above the makeshift altar was finished in a high gloss varnish similar to the tables at Cracker Barrel. The congregation was arranged in two blocks of folding chairs. Many of the men wore jeans and short sleeve white shirts with a tie. A few had chosen overalls. The women all wore dresses.

—Jacob Hall, "Behold, I Give You the Power"

# Chapter 13

Trion, Alabama
Saturday, September 14, 2019
4:30 p.m.

We're not out of the cemetery before she asks, "What was that Samson stuff about? These folks have given you enough shit about divorcing him without you dumping on yourself. What were you thinking?"

"I wasn't."

"When you wing it in class, I hope you do a better job."

"Are you finished?"

"For now."

"I'll try, Mom."

We both laugh, but I can't explain where Samson came from without telling her about my final phone call with Jacob. And I need someone on my side tonight. Someone who doesn't think I'm a snooty bitch.

"Let's stop at the house. I need to check on Willy." Stopping to see about Willy is a convenient break from everybody else. I've known Cindy almost as long as I've known Jacob. Her dad was a Cooper Tires salesman and her mom taught first grade. Because she was two years ahead, we weren't close friends until we moved back. With Jacob's crowd, I was usually with him. We were a couple. I thought he just wanted to keep me to himself, which is true. Now I realize that he probably wanted to keep his life compartmentalized for his own satisfaction.

"The first time Jacob brought you to one of our parties was shocking," Cindy says. "We knew who you were, Mike's little sister. But no one really knew you. We were juniors, and we didn't talk to freshmen as a rule. Not adults like us. Y'all were kids. We wanted Jacob for ourselves, and it annoyed the shit out of us, especially me, that he even asked you. We were the class of '72, a bunch of smart bad asses like Trion had never seen. How could he dare bring a lowly ninth grader among us?"

"I was nervous when Jacob asked me to go with him."

"When I first spoke to you, I doubt I was sweet," Cindy says.

"No, you weren't sweet. You weren't a bitch, either."

"Anybody with half a brain could tell he was smitten. He held your hand most of the night."

"I told Jacob I had to ask Mike if I could go."

"Why?"

"I was afraid what Mike might say, so Jacob asked him if he was okay with our dating."

"If your brother knew where that night would lead, he would've said 'hell no,'" she adds.

"When Jacob first came up to me while I waited for Algebra class, I was suspicious. If I'd seen or read *Carrie*, I'd have thought it was a setup."

"We would have used chicken blood," Cindy laughs.

Before opening the door, we hear Willy's whimpers. He jumps from one paw to the other, wagging his tongue in excitement to see us. "Good boy," I say, petting his head and heading for the kitchen.

"Want a beer or something stronger? I'm having a shot in my Coke."

"That sounds good," Cindy says, sitting down at the table, Willy's nails tapping the floor around her.

I pull out two tall, cold bottles of Coca-Cola from the fridge and a bottle of Jim Beam from the shelf above. Taking a swig from each Coke, I pour the bourbon in the bottles, some trickling down the side. Even when my hands aren't shaky, I don't have a very accurate aim.

If Jacob wasn't drinking a Miller, he drank bourbon and Coke, usually late at night when we'd gone through a couple of six packs. After Susan told me about his death, I drove to the state store and bought Jim Beam. Since our divorce, I've become a Jack Daniels girl, but Jacob's brand seems right for his goodbye. The bourbon's warm, sliding down like a consolation prize.

We carry our Cokes outside as Willy runs into the yard.

"I'd been talking to Jacob about his moving back here," I say.

"When?"

"Next year after he retired."

"Why did you ask him to come back?

"I'm lonely. I wanted someone to share time with, and I love Jacob."

"But you said no to taking care of him."

"That was long ago. I wanted to define myself apart from Jacob, and I did. Through teaching."

"You changed. He didn't."

"Given all our years together, why does it matter? He was my flawed lover. I was his. And the sex was still good. He paid attention to detail."

"I could use some attention," Cindy says.

Willy stands in front of her, big watery eyes looking almost into hers. She reaches down with both arms, hugs him around the neck, and pulls him closer.

"I guess you can go home again. We have," she says.

I walk back into the house, put our bottles next to the sink, and fill the bowl with Kibbles and Bits. Then I take dry food to Rhoda in the bedroom.

Talking to Cindy, I wind up lying. I'm not sure why. Maybe it's my persistent self-doubt. Of all the folks from Trion class of '72, she's the one person I should tell the deepest truth.

Settled in his ways, Jacob was more interested in his writing than anything else, though I never doubted that he loved me as much as he could love another human being. He was fenced in by his own words. He was the kind of guy who espoused feminism and thought he was progressive while expecting his wife to be a wife.

I lie down, close my eyes, and try to purge "was" from my mind.

"It's about time to go," Cindy says.

"I hate this, Cindy. I don't want Jacob dead."

"No one does," she says, sitting on the bed. "He rarely worried about appearances. Most of the time, he just did what he felt right. The boys used to call me Little Orphan Annie and at our first boy-girl mixer in sixth grade, I was the only girl sitting while everybody else danced. When Jacob saw me, he waved. On the second song, he asked if I wanted to be his partner. We danced the rest of the night."

"That was so Jacob."

I get off the bed, walk into the kitchen, and drink straight from the bottle.

They looked country. An expression I never heard up north, yet often bandied about in the small southern town where my college was located. A tall man was strumming an old SG that seemed out of place. He should have been playing a Telecaster or a Gretsch Country Gentleman, not the Gibson guitar Pete Townsend played and smashed in the early days of The Who. The woman at the Casio keyboard fit my idea of a rural church organist with her long hair and denim dress. But none of this I consciously saw when I opened that door.

—Jacob Hall, "Behold, I Give You the Power"

# Chapter 14

The Smith House
Saturday, September 14, 2019
5:00 p.m.

Cars are parked everywhere at Susan and Larry's: in the driveway and on Sycamore Lane, bumper to bumper on both sides. I'm glad I changed to flats. In the front yard, people are mingling. The faces look much more familiar and defined than they did at the funeral. There's the 1971 Trion football team, in dark pants, without their ties and jackets, huddled together, probably sharing stories about Jacob.

Catching me by the arm, Paul gives me the eye. "Come talk to us, girl. What are you drinking?" Thanks to Jim Beam, I smile as best I can. On a Friday night long ago, we were all at the Dairy Queen, Jacob and I snuggling when Paul blurted, "Get outta here. We know about you two."

Today I join Paul and the other guys. "I'd like bourbon and Coke."

"Just like the old days," he says and goes into the house.

A fine day for a wake, I think, as the guys continue talking like I'm not here. Even today with Jacob gone, lying in a box underground, they talk about work and money, how their wives spend it. I shift from one leg to the other, waiting for the bourbon that will help cloud reality, help me pretend I'm somewhere I'm not.

"Here, Miss Shakespeare." Paul hands me a tall glass that smells of butterscotch and tastes sweet, and I join the conversation.

"I haven't heard 'Miss Shakespeare' since high school," I say.

"You and Jacob were always the bookworms, reading shit I couldn't understand."

"He taught me how," I lie, stirring the ice with my finger. I was reading books of literary worth when I met him. That was the key reason he noticed me, what attracted him. But when people die, you want to contribute to their myth, stoke their story full of phenomenon. And I come to praise Jacob.

Paul drapes his arm over my shoulder and dangles his fingers to cop a feel.

"I better head inside," I say and twist my shoulder out of his reach.

"Hang in there," he says, trying to pat me on the butt, and I back away. The guys are already in their cups, giving them an excuse to take liberties. In my cups, too, I want to squeeze Paul's balls and crack them like paper-shell pecans.

In the South during the fall, football takes precedence Friday night and Saturday afternoon and evening, no matter what else happens. The crowd watches the game in the living room as the Tide leads by six points in the second quarter against the Gamecocks. Though my undergrad degree came from Bama, my Master's in English came from USC, and I consider South Carolina my true alma mater, much to Mike's displeasure.

Susan and Larry's living room, like their whole house, is a showplace. Wood floors with Oriental rugs, a burgundy velvet couch with two Queen Anne chairs to match, a cherry coffee table, and sliding glass doors that open onto a screened porch overlooking the golf course. The walls are filled with oils of landscapes, oak trees, and barns that Susan and Jacob's mama painted. All dark colors, browns and blacks with an occasional blue or red. An interior decorator from Birmingham was imported to "consult" on the house, and I wonder what she thought of the art.

Cindy's talking to Leann, standing close, laughing and nodding like good friends, but Cindy doesn't give a damn for her and probably is probing for gossip. In the kitchen, Susan arranges squares of cheddar and Jack cheese, impaled with fancy frilled toothpicks.

"How's Willy?" she asks.

"Not quite settled in. He's having to adjust to Rhoda."

Susan looks and sounds like the sister of the departed. Her eyes are swollen and red, her voice sandpaper rough. Even still she's dressed like a model in black chiffon with lace inlay on the bodice and a single strand of pearls.

"Jacob loved Willy almost as much as he loved you."

I shake my glass, ice ringing against the sides. She wants me to say something sweet about Jacob, some loving thing he did for me.

"I'm surprised folks from Illinois State aren't here."

"They're having a memorial next weekend. Larry and I are flying up."

Crystal walks in from the garage with a Coke bottle and opens it with an old-fashioned opener that we used to call a church key. There was little of Jacob to see in Crystal. Her eyes were more like Susan's and her bone structure, her high cheekbones, more like Larry's.

"Would you take these into the living room, Delilah?" Susan says and hands me the platter of cheese and crackers. "I always knew your tricks."

I start to breathe deeply and count to ten.

"I'll help," Crystal says.

The buffet in the dining room is already loaded with country ham, biscuits, funeral potatoes, sausage balls, cheddar cheese straws, deviled eggs, some of Leann's pimento cheese sandwiches, and toasted pecans. There's no room on the table. Crystal rearranges the dishes so I can leave the platter.

"Thanks, Crystal."

"You're welcome, Aunt Janet."

"You know I'm really not your aunt."

"I like calling you aunt except on campus."

"Just don't call me ma'am."

"Deal," she says and glances down before blurting, "Why does everybody put Uncle Jacob on a pedestal?"

I point to two needlepoint chairs for us to sit in the far corner.

"His kids don't," I reply.

"They're his kids," Crystal says.

"When people die, those of us left behind try to remember what was best about them. Don't speak ill of the dead is a cliché, and sometimes we need our clichés."

"Why did you and Uncle Jacob divorce?"

How much do I tell her? Was he smothering me? Or was I just eager to be on my own?

"I was tired."

"Of what?"

"Of being his student. Jacob was always going inside his head, leaving me to wait outside. That's what writers do. And I wanted to find my own world."

"You couldn't with Uncle Jacob?"

"Not then. Maybe I could have ten years after the divorce. Not earlier. There was too much of him. Not enough of me."

"I'm not sure I understand," Crystal says.

"I'm not sure I do either."

"I love his writing, but why are all his characters so … ," Crystal begins.

"Sad?" I say for her.

"Fucked up," she replies.

"Because he was a writer and saw things we didn't. He couldn't not write about what he witnessed."

"I want to be a writer. Don't tell Mom."

"Your secret's safe with me." I smile.

She laughs and heads to the porch. I join Cindy and Leann.

"What are you girls snickering about?" I ask. My tone's sassy, like that of my teenage self when Mother would quiz me about Jacob.

Cindy winks. "Leann's sharing sex secrets."

"My Lord, girl, everybody can hear you," Leann says.

"Everybody already knows," I say.

"What do you mean?" she asks.

"You know, Leann, your …."

"Sex appeal?" she finishes.

I smile and glance at Cindy who looks at Leann.

"Because Jacob and I slept together, you've always hated me," she says.

"I know about that night."

"What about that senior year?"

Feeling I could slap her right there at Jacob's wake in front of the Trion crowd, I glare at her. Blood would fly over her face, mixing red with mascara streaks. Jacob was no saint, though early on I tried to turn him into one. Now I want to turn Leann into the scapegoat. Furious, I spill my drink on her linen dress. Every last drop. She lets out a yelp and begins shaking her skirt as if it were on fire, the black hiding any stain of bourbon.

"Look what you've done," she screams.

"Sorry. My hands are shaky," I say and return with a dishtowel to clean up the spill.

Drying the front of her skirt with another dishtowel, Leann asks, "Why did you pour your drink on me? No bullshit about shaky hands."

"I don't want to hear about Jacob sleeping around, today especially."

"Why take out your feelings on me?" Leann asks. "I'm tired of you treating me like trash."

"I don't."

"You do. You've been back two years and act too good for me whenever I run into you."

We walk back to the kitchen. She pours bourbon over her ice, and I get a glass of water.

My head is splitting. Leann's right. I tend to dismiss her as a 50s down-home girl with a high school diploma and three kids.

Nobody else is in the kitchen, and I blurt out, "I've always been a little, maybe a lot, jealous. I knew Jacob was attracted to you."

Larry comes in and sees us at the table. "Hey," he says. Not saying a word, we both turn. "See you later," and he walks back to the game.

"He married you," she says and finishes her drink, reaching for a pimento cheese sandwich. "And you divorced him."

"I finally couldn't handle Jacob sleeping with other women," I say.

"If you didn't want him sleeping around, why did you let him go?"

"Regardless of whether he was married, he was going to."

Leann pulls a pack of cigarettes from her purse and goes to the backyard.

I see her alone, at the fence.

Susan and Larry have a backyard big enough for an Olympic pool. Considering his financial success, I'm surprised by how plain they leave the back, particularly compared to the front with its trimmed hedges and Pick's Garden Center flowers. There's a short breezeway onto an expanse of carefully manicured crabgrass. No trees, no flowers. A carpet of green fenced off from the golf course. I figure they aren't worried about what golfers, focused on their game, think about the yard. The front yard, in view of passing traffic, is another place to show their wealth.

When I reach Leann, two golfers are getting back into their cart.

"That's the dumbest fucking game," she says.

"I don't know. There's a certain elegance to it. A Zen quality."

"Bobby would get up Sunday mornings and leave me with three little kids. He'd come home drunk after drinking in the clubhouse with the boys. He'd drop into his recliner and watch football until he fell asleep, mouth open and snoring loud enough to wake the dead. I'd put the kids to bed and take a long bath, knowing I'd be sound asleep before he made it to bed."

"You two seemed happy in high school," I say.

"We were. Then I got pregnant, we got married, and it wasn't a year before he started fucking around with whoever. I might have erred in high school but once I had that ring on my finger, I was good as gold. Then he up and decided being a dad wasn't for him and found a cute girl ten years younger. He left me and the kids without a care to how we survived. He was always late with child support and the judge, a friend of Bobby's dad, didn't award much alimony because I was young and able-bodied."

"That must have been hell," I say.

"It was. With no college and little work experience, I couldn't do much. I waited tables at The Food Basket then took a job at The Lunch

Box. The owner said she'd pay me minimum wage plus tips."

"How'd you manage with the kids?"

"They were great. Ages six, seven, and nine when Bobby left. They pitched in with the housekeeping and did what they could. After about ten years of waiting tables and taking over management, I scraped up the money to buy the place when Florence wanted to sell and move to Gulf Shores. The kids did fine. Two went to college, and all have good jobs."

"Are you a grandmother?"

"Two times over," Leann says, showing me photos on her phone.

With their blue eyes and full lips, the kids favor Leann. "They're lovely. Look a lot like you."

Still scrolling through her pictures, she smiles.

Off and on through the years, I've wondered how a child from Jacob and me would look. Whose genes would have dominated?

"I always envied you. Jacob loved you to pieces. I thought Bobby loved me. He just didn't have what Jacob had. He liked to be with us girls, treated us like equals."

"A lot of the time," I reply. "But he wanted a wife, and not just someone to take care of the home. He wanted someone to take care of him. What he really wanted was to write. He'd vanish into his writing for hours on end."

"Jacob seemed too young for a heart attack," Leann says.

"Fore," someone yelled, and a white golf ball flew over our heads.

"I guess that's why Susan and Larry don't have a pool," I say.

"That's why everybody's out front drinking," Leann says and hands me the ball.

"Larry has a trash can full of these in the garage."

Ignoring the cries of the ball's owner, she turns and waves over her shoulder. We go back to the kitchen, and I drop the golf ball in a bowl of Red Delicious apples on the counter.

"I'm going to find Cindy," I say, stopping at the door and looking back at Leann. "Those sandwiches are good."

"How would you know? You didn't eat any," she replies.

What I saw was Georgia in her yellow dress with small red flowers. Don't ask me what kind. I've never been good at botany or biology or herpetology. But I know a fucking rattlesnake when I see one, and she was holding a three-foot rattler in her hands and dancing with her eyes closed in what can only be called rapture. I froze. Unable to speak or move. The need to urinate spread across my crotch.
—Jacob Hall, "Behold, I Give You the Power"

# Chapter 15

The Smith House
Saturday, September 14, 2019
5:30 p.m.


Cindy's smoking a cigarette with Charlie, quarterback on the '71 Aggies. He and Jacob both grew up on chicken farms and shared a good-ole-boy bond. And they both defied the jock stereotype by being smart guys who studied and went on to college. Charlie became an internist and set up practice in Trion.

"Why are you in the front yard?"

"Why, why, why Delilah," Charlie sings in a husky, baritone voice, taking the cigarette from Cindy, who smacks him upside the head."

"Piss off the Baptists," she says.

"Sorry," Charlie says.

"You ought to be," I say.

"How are you holding up?" he asks and passes the cigarette back to Cindy.

"Not well if I hear those lyrics again. Should you be smoking?"

"I'm not. Cindy is," he says with a bourbon grin.

"I'm the culprit. He's going to retire," Cindy says.

"What will you do?" I ask.

"Play more golf, drink more liquor."

"Here's to Jacob," Cindy says. We tap our glasses together and hear a roar from the house.

"I need to go see where my wife is."

We watch him disappear into football fans.

"That boy's got his tail between his legs," Cindy says.

"Did you sleep with Jacob?" I ask.

"No!"

"Did he ever ask you?"

"No. Otherwise, I would have."

"Besides Leann, whom did he fuck? Linda?" I point to the redhead in a blue suit and stiletto heels.

"God, Janet. Why ask me?"

"You were a cheerleader."

"Why would I keep tabs on who slept with Jacob? Why don't you ask Leann? Anyway, why does it matter? That was almost fifty years ago."

I hold up my empty glass and turn toward the house.

"Where are you going?" Cindy asks.

"Back inside."

Mike's wife walks out the door, and there's no way to avoid her. She stops when she sees me.

"Are you okay?" she asks.

"What do you think?"

Mary Jane opens her purse, a shocking pink with a gold shoulder chain and gold clasp, designer initials on the flap. She pulls out her keys, and I wonder if the bag costs more than our first car.

"Are you ever going to sell that house? It won't be worth much if you wait too long. Never seemed right that Grace left it to you since Mike took care of her, taking her to doctor appointments, picking up her drugs, buying groceries. Whatever she needed doing, he did it. Where were you?"

"Far away doing things that made Aunt Grace proud. I'm her namesake and think she wanted me to come back to Trion to carry on good works. Someone has to explain why so much of this is just wrong." I spread my arms to indicate this nouveau neighborhood.

"You're such a little brat. I thought you were a brat in high school, too," Mary Jane says and walks off.

Used to her resentment, I usually deal with it by seeing her as little as possible. I don't look forward to the eventual lecture from my brother about my manners. Since she's the one swearing, maybe she won't mention our exchange.

Pouring myself a Coke in the kitchen, I don't see Leann so follow the noise to the television. The crowd shouts at the screen. South Carolina has stopped Bama on the third and short.

"Go Cocks," I yell.

The crowd turns, offers derisive rejoinders like *Traitor. Go back to South Carolina, you low country idiot.* Bama goes for it on the fourth down and gains nine yards.

I wonder how many of these women mourning Jacob fucked him.

But why do I care? It's ancient history, almost half a century. Yet, betrayal leaves a lingering wound. Perhaps I'm trying to diminish Jacob to lessen the guilt I feel. But he didn't deserve to die from fucking around and my power play was just the petty meanness of trying to even the score. Why do we wound those we love? And why am I such a shit? Mary Jane was being kind, especially for her, and I had to be a smart ass. All of these folks miss Jacob. Many loved him.

Seeing Nora on the porch alone, I walk to the door. Still lovely in a fragile way like Richardson's *Clarissa*, she looks as if the last thirty years haven't worn on her except around the eyes. Then those eyes turn to me.

"Can I join you?" I ask.

Nora nods.

I sit in the wicker rocker across from her.

"Must be nice," I say.

"Nothing nice about this," she replies, staring at me.

"I mean having kids. Where are the girls?"

"Off with Crystal. You didn't want kids. They weren't part of the feminist stance you took."

"I didn't. Though sometimes when I see a mother and daughter …."

"You wish you had one," Nora finishes.

"Today especially. It's difficult to believe Jacob's gone."

"For you maybe. He was always gone for us."

I shake my glass; the diminishing ice barely knocks. Groans come from the living room. "Shit, interception," someone says. "Go Cocks," I say, eliciting a smile from Nora.

"He wanted kids."

"He thought he did," Nora replies.

"What do you mean?"

"During my pregnancy, he brought home chocolate ice cream and massaged my belly. We still made love."

I look away, eyes moist.

"My breasts filled, and I was always aroused."

"Why are you telling me this?"

"There was a time," and Nora pushes her sleeves to her elbow, "when I thought it was just Jacob and me."

"It was just Jacob and you."

"It was never just us. You were always there, always in the middle of whatever we did. You read everything he wrote. I would have, but he didn't ask me. He asked you and told me what you thought. Janet said this, Janet liked that."

"Nora, even before our divorce, he wanted you."

"Not really. He wanted a wifey. I was just too naïve and in love with love to see it."

Wrapping the napkin around my glass, I lower my head.

"And you won the lottery," I say.

"Until the twins came. Then he stayed at school most of the time, claiming he couldn't write at home. He wasn't interested in family life."

"Neither was I when you came between us," I reply.

"I was just there at the wrong time."

In the living room, noise explodes. Bama scores another touchdown against Carolina, and everybody's jumping and hugging. We watch them while the September sun begins to fade.

"Writing was his true love," I say.

Nora pulls back and studies me, an animal at the zoo.

"Are you really so naïve?" she asks. "He wrote everything for you. He never really left you. You ruined our marriage before it even started. I was just his broodmare." She leans against the porch swing and closes her eyes.

I have no defense, no witty response, no comforting reply.


Columbia, South Carolina
Friday, May 7, 1982
7:30 p.m.


I never thought of Nora until the night of Dr. Griener's year-end party. He and Jacob were talking when Nora, Dr. Greiner's student assistant and a sophomore English major, walked into the room. I was on the couch chatting with Ana, another grad student, who'd gone for a couple of beers while I watched Jacob throw his arm over Nora's shoulder. A playful gesture typical of Jacob, his arm stayed there a little too long. Dr. Greiner left. Jacob moved closer, his head leaning into hers, nearly touching. They were looking at the photo of Dr. Greiner in hospital garb, holding his infant son, when Nora turned and said something to Jacob. They broke into laughter then walked onto the patio.

Ana stepped in front of me with the beer. "Here," she said, handing one to me as I slid over.

"Are you going to take the Woolf seminar next semester?" she asked.

I looked out the patio door.

"Are you taking the Woolf seminar?" she asked again.

"Sorry. Wouldn't miss it. I love *A Room of One's Own*."

"Makes you wonder why we put up with the patriarchy."

"Sex?" I squirmed as she moved closer, her leg touching mine.

"Then you haven't read *Mrs. Dalloway*," she said.

I looked at her, black hair almost to her waist and a near flawless complexion except for a few acne scars above the right corner of her mouth.

"Woolf makes me want to fuck Sally Seton," she said.

"Not sure Jacob would like that," I said, playing with my ring.

"What's Jacob got to do with it?" she asked.

I held up my left hand, adorned with a simple gold band.

"I did my senior thesis on Woolf. Virginia married Leonard though her passion was for women," Ana said and smiled at my obvious discomfort.

Taking off my sweater and crossing my legs, jeans pressed against my crotch, I felt my face flush. I suspected she, twisting strands of hair tight around her finger, noticed.

"I want to find Jacob," I said, standing up.

"Did I frighten you?"

Touching her on the arm, I let my hand linger in response until I left her on the couch and walked into the open air. Green and pink paper lanterns were strung, glowing like giant fireflies. Next to the picnic table was a stainless-steel keg on ice. Jacob was nowhere in sight. I stood there long enough to finish my beer and start another. Someone said "hey" and I turned to see Ana.

"Need a ride?"

"Maybe," I said and walked through the crowd. Still no Jacob. I went back where Ana waited, holding my sweater.


Columbia, South Carolina
Saturday, May 8, 1982
8:30 a.m.


The next morning Jacob was at the table, drinking coffee and reading when I got home. He looked up, eyes streaked red.

"Where've you been?" he asked.

"Ana's. When I couldn't find you or the car, she offered me a ride."

"You had a sleepover?"

"Stopped at her place for a beer. I called and let the phone ring ten times."

"I stayed late."

"I looked for you on the patio."

"Nora and I went to the gazebo."

"Why?"

"She wanted to talk English, and the music was too loud."

I reached in the cabinet for two Tylenol and poured myself a cup of coffee. It still had a crisp, sharp taste, not yet burned. I added some milk.

"How long have you been up?"

"Long enough to make coffee," he said, returning to the paper. His hair was wet.

He was quieter than usual; his voice seemed uninterested. His eyes evaded mine. I knew Jacob's manner when not in control, his habit of avoidance. And I remembered him with Nora, his arm on her shoulder, their talking close. And I remembered Ana, how warm she felt.

"I'm going to shower," I said. Pulling back the curtain, I was surprised to find it dry, no wetness on the tiles. I turned on the water and closed my eyes, tilting my face upward, letting water wash over my head and down my body. I stood in the cascade and cleansed myself of any musk from the night before. Hearing the rings scrape across the rod, I felt Jacob's hand on my arm. He moved next to me, and our bodies pressed together. Paying more attention to each other than normal, we made love in a guilty way,

The rest of the day, we barely spoke. He retreated to the bedroom to write. On the couch, I read *Mrs. Dalloway*. I sensed that we both knew we'd cheated on each other. For me, it didn't quite feel like cheating. No penis penetration. Bill Clinton's comment that he didn't have sex with Monica Lewinsky always made some sense. "No penis penetration" meant no sex. I justified being with another woman as a political act, challenging the patriarchy. Of course, now that position seems insulting and like complete bullshit. I knew Jacob was going to fuck Nora, and I wanted to keep the stakes even. I could have found the car and waited. I could have really searched for him.

There's a thing that I do, and I suspect others do: we separate what we know from what we admit to ourselves. I knew we were in decline though I didn't want us to be. No, that's not quite true. I wanted Jacob to evolve and stay the same, which was idiotic. Thus, I fucked my Sally Seton.

A man, Uncle John I assumed, pulled a thicker, longer snake from
a wooden box. This snake had a pattern of diamonds down the back.
Uncle John turned and offered it to the congregation. No one came
forward. He held the snake high above him.
—Jacob Hall, "Behold, I Give You the Power"

# Chapter 16

The Smith House
Saturday, September 14, 2019
5:47 p.m.

I don't want to believe Nora. I want to hold to my belief that Jacob
wrote for himself. For immortality. In search of the perfect language, he
was the artist. Otherwise, I am the monster who stole his birthright,
smothered his voice. If Jacob wrote ultimately to please me, what pain
did I inflict? What pressure?
"Will you help me with the coffee?" Susan gestures for me to follow.
"What were you and Nora chatting about?"
"Nothing much."
"Before the silence. Don't think I wasn't keeping an eye on you."
"Jacob."
"What about Jacob?"
"Nora accused me of ruining their marriage."
Reaching into the fridge, Susan pulls out a platter of crudités, celery
and carrot sticks, spring onions, sliced red peppers, and radishes
heaped around a bowl of spinach dip.
I take a carrot and lightly drag it across the top of the dip, trying not
to leave a visible trace. "A touch of Tabasco. This tastes like Jacob's. You
must have made it."
"What else did she say?"
"Why do you care?"
Susan starts putting dirty plates into the sink.
"Just wondering if the ex-wives club speaks ill of the dead."
"No. Only fond memories."
Holding a couple of empty glasses, Paul walks in and fills them with
ice. Then he reaches for the Jim Beam, brushing my breasts. Swatting
him with my hand, I quietly mumble, "Fuck you."

"Commercial break. Bama's up by fourteen," he says and leaves.

"Tell me what Nora said about Jacob," Susan says.

"Why?" I pop a radish in my mouth. Then another.

"You and Jacob talked a lot."

"So?"

"Was he happy?"

"Always down about something."

She pulls out more sandwiches, and I grab one from the top.

"The older he got, the more self-loathing. Moaned about rejection," I say.

"When did you last talk?"

"The night he died. But he always kept secrets." I remember passing off his raspier voice to a long day at school.

"Didn't he tell you everything?"

"Does Larry tell you everything?"

"I wish he wouldn't. So boring."

"Pass these around," she says and hands me stacks of peanut butter cookies.

Everyone in the living room stares at the screen: Bama on the ten-yard line. In her stocking feet, Cindy stands by Mike, who wears a red T-shirt with Roll Tide across his chest, and Ken's next to them. I look for Barbara, who's nowhere in sight.

"Time for sweets," I break in.

Without turning away from the game, Cindy and Mike grab a cookie.

"I like anything sweet," Ken says, taking two.

"I know." I smile.

He bites into his cookie then holds it out for me.

"Where's the Missus?"

"Home with a migraine."

I lean in and bite. With his lanky build and cleft chin, blue eyes and snaggle tooth, he has a look that appeals.

"Are you always in a hurry?" he asks.

"Only when I'm hungry."

"You okay?"

"No. Back to work."

Annoying the fans, I weave through the crowd.

"That bird's cooked," Charlie says.

Laughing, I hand him a cookie. At the buffet, Crystal loads a napkin with pimento cheese sandwiches and country ham biscuits.

"Want a cookie?"

"Yes," she answers, grabbing four then walking down the hall to her suite, the woody smell of dope trailing her. Her cousins Ruth and Jane sit to the side near the front window. They move with the slow, steady pace of the stoned. The last time I got high was with their dad at a Modern Language Conference. He rolled a fat joint, and we passed it back and forth, sitting on the floor of his hotel room and singing "American Pie." He was the only person I ever knew who could sing all the lyrics from memory while I chimed in on the chorus.

His girls look a bit tousled, eyes smeared black, and blonde hair pulled back in curly ponytails. Identical twins, they seem unaware of exuding sex. Whispering behind their hands when I appear with cookies, they nab a handful and never glance my way.

The kids Jacob always wanted: smart, funny, assured, and, as he said, shaped by Nora. He frequently told me that he felt like a third wheel, the stereotypically maligned father who was never there and just stepped into their lives occasionally for winter and summer visits.

"Your dad spoke of you often," I say.

Neither look up.

Raising my voice, I repeat, "Your dad spoke of you often."

Finally, they turn, eyes bloodshot.

"He spoke of you often, too," Ruth says.

"That's the problem—or was," Jane says.

I want them to like me. They're his blood.

"Your dad was complicated."

"Probably would have been a lot less if you'd disappeared," Ruth says.

"That would've helped," Jane says.

"He wanted to name her Janet," Ruth says, hugging Jane.

"Mom refused. It's bad enough bearing most of your name," Jane says.

My body comes over cold. I want to say something to pierce their armor, shake them up, make them realize I'm not who they think I am. Nonetheless, I stand in guilt. Maybe I'm exactly who they think I am: the woman who never let their father go. How simple it would have been never to answer his calls, to ignore his emails. Is my grief for the passing of Jacob or for the passing of my hold over him? No more late-night calls, no more hideaways. No more power over Jacob.

"We don't need extra cookies," Ruth says.

Coming out of the kitchen, Nora motions to them. Ruth takes Jane's hand, and they start toward the door when Jane turns to whisper in my ear, "He shot himself."

They join their mother, and the three walk out.

Georgia swayed with her snake. The tall guy with the SG played a devilish lick. The scene was unreal. Clipped from some independent film that would make the smaller festival circuit in hope the streaming services would pick it up. Uncle John played by Tommie Lee Jones or Robert Duvall, Georgia by some TV star wanting to move into movies, and me by the arrogant writer-director of the film.

—Jacob Hall, "Behold, I Give You the Power"

# Chapter 17

Columbia, South Carolina
Thursday, December 11, 1980
11:30 p.m.

On the floor in front of the fireplace, we watched flames dance and pop to the rhythm of the room's draft. Final essays from our writing classes were stacked on the kitchen table, and on top of each pile were the grading sheets to be turned in Monday. Three weeks of break lay ahead. No students. No papers to grade. No papers to write. Our only obligation was to drive back to Trion for Christmas.

"Here's to another semester of freshman papers past," Jacob said as he rang his bottle neck on mine. We each drank a six-pack of Miller, slogging through essays, and he made a run to the 7-Eleven for whatever Miller was available, quarts, cans, bottles.

"Why do we always get drunk after grading?" I asked, my foot touching his leg, slowly moving up from the ankle.

"Because we can," Jacob said.

Turning away from the fire, I looked at him, his face red, and wondered if he was too drunk for sex. With my foot, I gave him a little shove. He just smiled and drank more beer.

"On one of my essays is a note from Nora. I told you about her. She's applied to be Dr. Greiner's student assistant."

"And?" I asked.

"She wants to know why she has to read stories by crazy people."

"What crazy people?"

"Woolf."

"Which story?"

"'The Mark on the Wall.' She doesn't think we should read it because Woolf committed suicide."

"What a rube. Did she complain about Hemingway?"

"Nope."

We sat drinking our beer. I was pissed about how the female students were so male defined. If you can't fucking convince women of the oppressive patriarchy, how can you convince men?

"Did you answer her?"

"I wrote that suicide is a human right."

I rolled over and put my head in Jacob's lap. He just kept looking into the fire.

"What are you thinking?"

"I'm trying to remember the lyrics to the *Mash* theme," he said and started humming.

Following along and taking pleasure in this lighter turn, I joined him. Jacob stopped and looked down at me, then we kissed. Enjoying the beery taste of his tongue, I closed my eyes.

"No matter what happens, writers have the final power," he said.

I began to rub his leg. "What are you talking about?"

"Their power over life."

"Woolf drowned herself, Plath stuck her head in an oven, Hemingway blew his off," I said.

"Exactly. They controlled their ending. No matter what, we're our own creators."

"Jacob, they all suffered from some form of depression. Their final act was tragic."

He took a tall drink. "I see their suicides as heroic. Woolf faced another extended stay in an asylum, and Plath was burdened with two babies, whom she loved. Still, they crowded out her writing."

"I doubt if Ted Hughes helped," I said. "And Hemingway?"

"He saw himself getting old, his writing losing the appeal it once had, and he concluded himself. He pulled on that barrel as he lived his life, with intention and passion. He was a hero," Jacob said.

I looked up at Jacob. He stared into the fire and started humming again.

When I felt too intoxicated to argue with him, I played my part in what I called "midnight meanderings." Looking back now, I see myself complicit in his romanticizing suicide. Why didn't I call Jacob out? Call it a selfish and loveless act? Take a stand for Plath's babies and Woolf's husband? Hemingway's sons? Why didn't I hear the fear in Jacob's voice?

Those thoughts helped me settle into this alien world until a convulsion shook Georgia and her eyes, her blue-green eyes, opened, and she looked at me.

—Jacob Hall, "Behold, I Give You the Power"

# Chapter 18

The Smith House
Saturday, September 14, 2019
6:30 p.m.

"You plan to eat *all* the cookies?" Cindy asks.

Handing her the platter, I hurry to the bathroom down the hall from Crystal's room and barely make it to the toilet before vomiting. The sour smell of pimento cheese mixed with the fragrant potpourri of dead roses on the toilet tank top nauseate me even greater. Hovering over the bowl, I grip it for dear life, then reach up and flush when someone knocks.

"Occupied."

"Okay in there?" Cindy asks.

"I'll live."

"If you need me, I'm out front."

On my knees, I imagine Jacob's body sprawled on a wooden floor, his dad's pistol still in his hand. Blood pooling around his head, and Willy crying for Jacob to sit up, clean the mess.

*I'm back in court. Susan's lawyer has additional questions.*

*Susan's Lawyer: Ms. Hall, we have new information. It's possible that Jacob Hall shot himself. Do you think that is feasible?*

*Janet: I don't know.*

*Susan's Lawyer: Did he ever discuss suicide with you?*

*Janet: Yes. Back in graduate school. One night when we were drinking.*

*Susan's Lawyer: And what was his opinion?*

*Janet: He thought it was an act of bravery. That Hemingway was brave to end his life when he could no longer write.*

*Susan's Lawyer: An act of bravery. Do you agree?*

*Janet: No. You need to consider the damage killing yourself inflicts on those left behind.*

*Susan's Lawyer: Did you share your opinion with Jacob?*

*Janet: I told him Hemingway suffered from depression.*

*Susan's Lawyer: But you didn't argue with him, did you? You were quite agreeable with Jacob back then.*

*Janet: No, I did not dispute him.*

*Susan's Lawyer: You spoke with Jacob the night he died.*

*Janet: Yes.*

*Susan's Lawyer: What did you talk about?*

*Janet: His writing.*

*Susan's Lawyer: Anything else?*

*Janet: I wanted him to move back to Trion. I thought we could be happy here.*

*Susan's Lawyer: Did Jacob agree with you?*

*Janet: No.*

*Susan's Lawyer: Did he tell you why?*

*Janet: He thought I should move up north or we should move to California.*

*Susan's Lawyer: But you didn't entertain those options. You wanted him to move here.*

*Janet: Yes.*

*Susan's Lawyer: Why?*

*Janet: He called me all the time. I edited his work. It would be easy. I already own a house. My brother and his sister live here.*

*Susan's Lawyer: How did your argument end?*

*Janet: I suggested we take a break.*

*Susan's Lawyer: How did Jacob respond?*

*Janet: He asked if I was threatening him.*

*Susan's Lawyer: Did you?*

*Janet: Yes. I told him, "Either you come back to Trion, or I'm done. Find someone else to hold your hand."*

*Susan's Lawyer: Hold his hand? Can you explain that comment?*

*Janet: Jacob never sent out any of his writing unless I told him it was finished.*

*Susan's Lawyer: Jacob was drunk. He had become dependent on you. He needed you to write. If you shut him off, then he wouldn't be able to write. Like Ernest Hemingway in the end. And it is quite possible that he followed Hemingway's example because of you.*

*Janet: Jacob had a heart attack.*

*Susan's Lawyer: Maybe. However, his daughter said he shot himself. At the wake and the funeral his sister had his casket sealed. So, Ms. Hall, if your threat didn't give him the heart attack, it's quite plausible that your threat caused him to kill himself. Either way, your actions caused the death of Jacob Hall. Do you accept that you are responsible?*

I flush the toilet again, turn on the fan, and search through the cabinets for some toothpaste. I find one of those small Delta kits that the airline gives passengers when luggage is lost. After splashing water on my face, brushing my teeth, and combing my hair, I inspect myself in the mirror and leave for Crystal's room. I tap on her door.

An incriminatingly long pause follows before the door opens, a crack revealing Crystal.

"May I come in for a minute?"

Opening it just enough for me to slip through, Crystal closes it quickly. The first thing I notice are the raised windows and the ceiling fan humming strong. Second, I'm struck by the bedroom's size, bigger than my living room, dining room, and kitchen combined. A room at the end of this house must be lonely.

"Are you all right, Aunt Janet?"

"I've been better. Did the twins talk to you about their dad?"

"No. They just wanted to get away from everybody."

"Did they mention anything about him?"

"No," she says, lowering her eyes.

"What did they say?"

"It's not important."

"Does your mom know you get high?"

Crystal tightens and says, "They called you a cunt."

"They may be right." I try to laugh. What comes out is something else, more like a stifled cry.

Looking around the room for her stash, I settle on an old white music box with gold plated trim, worn from too much handling over the years. When I open it, a ballerina pops up, though she doesn't pirouette. The weight is wrong. Where the works should be is a small bag with three neatly rolled joints.

"Did you buy this at school?" I ask.

"A friend gave it to me."

"I won't tell your mom, but I daresay she knows. My Aunt Grace used to hide her pot inside a hollowed copy of a book."

"What book?"

"You are Jacob's niece. *The Complete Poems* by Elizabeth Bishop."

"Want a piece of gum?" Crystal asks.

"Is my breath that bad?"

Nodding, Crystal turns to get her purse while I filch a joint and set the baggie back with the ballerina.

In the living room, the game's over. The guys from the 1971 Aggie football team, two of them with various stages of bald heads and the other two turned gray, huddle at the edge of Susan's yard, probably eager to go home, away from this dreadful mortality. One of theirs dead at sixty-six. A fallen Aggie. Ashes of death fall on everyone.

Heels in one hand with a drink and cigarette in the other, Cindy motions that she's ready to leave. To indicate I'm not, I hold up my thumb and forefinger and go find Susan.

The kitchen's full of ladies. Carrying clean casserole dishes, three wives in black nod on their way out. Two more follow, each with a Tupperware container of leftovers. My stomach rumbles its displeasure. With her heels kicked off and a clear drink, probably Grey Goose and water, Susan sits at the kitchen table. I pour myself some Coke and sit beside her.

"Long day," I say, reaching for a saltine. Except for the rattle of newly dispensed ice in the fridge, the kitchen's quiet.

"Now a long night," she replies.

"Jacob would've been pleased," I say.

"Most of his buddies were here," she says, rubbing her eyes.

We look straight ahead into the dusk. Breaking the silence, I crack ice between my teeth,

"Larry cringes when he hears you crack ice," she smiles.

"Jacob liked those guys, especially Charlie. But Jacob never felt like he belonged here."

"You're wrong," she says, rolling her chair back from the table and taking a long drink.

"Why do you think we didn't visit more?"

"You. You never seemed happy here."

"Did he and Nora ever visit?"

"They had kids," she says.

"What about after the divorce?"

Susan doesn't say a thing, just bumps her knees together.

"Jacob wasn't comfortable in Trion." My words sound shrill as if I were spitting them out, droplets falling in air.

"The problem was you got to him," she says.

"Me?"

"You got your talons in him."

"What?"

"After y'all started dating, he was never the same."

"He was two years older," I say.

"He did what you wanted," Susan replies and folds her arms over her stomach.

"I followed him to Tuscaloosa."

"After he stayed at Trion CC."

"What's your point?"

"He had a scholarship to the university. But you asked him to stay here until you finished high school."

I start swinging my right leg and remember that day in March Jacob told me about his scholarship. My sixteenth birthday. We were at the Catfish Café—the best fried fish in Davis County—a log cabin on the Tennessee River, orange and blue, crimson and white banners on the wall. When he told me, I began to cry. He said he'd come home every weekend. I said that wouldn't be enough. He didn't say another word about it until two weeks later when he said he turned it down.

"I won't lie. Not today. I wanted him to stay."

"You asked him to stay," Susan says.

"You think I changed him?"

"You know you did."

"If I had the ability to change him, I never would have left him."

"You can lie to yourself. You can't lie to me," she says.

Turning to face Susan, whose mascara is smeared charcoal, I ask, "Why didn't you tell me?"

"Tell you what?"

"What do you think?"

"I don't know what you're asking me," she says.

"That Jacob … took his own life."

"Nonsense. He died of a heart attack." Shifting her body, she presses hard against the back of the chair.

"That's not what Jane told me."

Susan pulls the plate of sandwiches toward her. "She's trying to hurt you. Those girls hate you."

"They don't know me," I say.

"They know all about the first wife."

"Tell me the truth. Why was the casket closed?"

"That's what Jacob wanted."

"He wanted to be cremated, ashes tossed into the wind."

"Why would I lie?" Susan asks.

"Because you don't want Trion to know the truth."

"I'm tired. Please leave and take that cake with you," she says and picks up her phone.

Dismissed, I rescue the cake from the garage refrigerator. When I return, Susan is gone. I glance out the window into the backyard. No shimmer of summer fireflies. In the dusk, the ninth-hole contours look like burial mounds.

My cool demeanor was flushed and replaced with the need to be back in the drunken dark. Away from harsh florescent lights and pulsating music. Safe from these serpents. But with the knowledge of what she's held and how she'd held it in pure belief.
—Jacob Hall, "Behold, I Give You the Power"

# Chapter 19

Columbia, South Carolina
Sunday, April 4, 1982
1:00 p.m.

I placed *Orlando* on the coffee table. Unaware, Jacob read on, lost in Faulkner just as Jacob became lost in his own writing. I could stand, leave the room, and walk out of the apartment. Chances were he'd never notice. He was present in that way. When he talked to you, however, you had his full attention. When he made love to you, you had his full attention. When he wrote, you disappeared.

"It's not working," I said.

He didn't hear me. I reached over and lowered the book and repeated myself.

"What's not working?"

"Us."

He held onto *Light in August*, his thumb holding his place.

"You're kidding," he said. "We have great sex. We don't argue."

"You're not here for me."

He smiled, probably thinking he could just fuck his way out of this.

"You write. I study."

Leaning toward me, his mouth slightly open, he uttered one word. "Okay."

"Then I cook our meals, wash our dishes and clothes, and clean the apartment."

"I take out the garbage and make the runs for pizza and beer," he said.

"Maybe if we'd stayed in Trion, I could have been your little angel in the house."

"Don't quote Woolf at me."

Putting the book down and turning his body to face me, his skin pale from too little sun, he reached down for his can of Coke.

"I can do more house stuff," he said.

"I can't find me because there's too much of you."

"You want me to be less of me?"

"No."

"I don't know if I even could. I haven't changed, Janet."

"I've changed," I said and pressed my fingers against my cheek, sliding them back and forth.

"So this is your fucking fault." he said.

"Yes," I said.

Jacob's words scheduled our life together, his time was precious and indeterminate. He would hole up for hours and find food on the table and me waiting to share whatever space he had left.

Like one of our professors, he raised his voice. "Lena Grove walked from Alabama to Mississippi to find Lucas Burch. She sacrificed for love."

"Don't quote Faulkner at me."

Jacob smiled, then his eyes filled with tears, and I could feel mine tearing up. Taking his hand, I led him to the bed, slipped off his clothes, and wrapped my arms around him. He lay still while I kissed his body and held him inside my mouth until he became hard. I moved on top, rising and falling, each time more intense, feeling as if I would split open. His eyes closed. He never closed his eyes when we were making love.

I cried as he came.

He fell asleep as I held him. Then I dressed and threw some clothes and essentials into my backpack, closing the door quietly behind me.

Georgia slowed and moved toward me. As she approached, she spoke to the serpent. The congregation's gaze followed her until she stood with her arms outstretched and offering the snake. Standing there, I wanted to be the child I once was. Safe in my room, the window cracked open to let the night air in, and shielded by prayer— *If I die before I wake, I pray the Lord my Soul to take.* But did I have a soul to take? And if I did, who would want such a soul?
—Jacob Hall, "Behold, I Give You the Power"

# Chapter 20

Starbucks
Trion, Alabama
Saturday, September 14, 2019
7:40 p.m.

Cindy and I stop at Starbucks. Evening customers are starting to collect. On both sides of the entry are communal tables for computers while tables for two run along the walls hung with watercolors and photographs of Sand Mountain, our sandstone plateau fifteen hundred feet above sea level. The only "coffee café" in town attracts an eclectic clientele of students, good-ole boys, wannabe hipsters, and local artists whose primarily black clothing matches our funeral attire.

Cindy grabs a table for two near the window while I walk to the counter flanked by baked goods on one side and on the other, busy baristas amidst the clink of blenders and grinding of ice. Bright lights bounce off the glass as if the day were just beginning.

"I'd like one tall house blend and one grandé cinnamon vanilla latte," I say to the woman who takes the order and passes it to the barista who writes our names and marks our drinks on the white and green cups.

Getting out my wallet, I ask her, "Do you mind if I share a cake with the clientele?"

"We're not supposed to let customers share food not bought here. What kind is it?"

"*Tres leches* from La Conchita."

"That's my favorite. Go ahead this time," she says and hands me a plastic wrapped knife, a bunch of forks, and a stack of napkins. "You can even make an announcement."

"Thanks so much. You're the best."

I see Amada sitting nearby with two other girls, both familiar faces, probably students at Trion CC, hunched over their computers.

"This is how you spend Saturday evening?" I ask.

"We have an American history paper due Monday," Amada says.

"I work on deadline and still pull all-nighters to grade research papers."

"I didn't know professors do that," another girl says.

"How was the funeral?" Amada asks.

"Very sad. I spoke first. My voice cracked the whole way through."

"My *abuela* died last year, and I feel like she passed yesterday. I cry every day." Wanting to say more, I reach down and hug Amada.

"Come to our table and get some *tres leches* when you break."

"That's what the napkins and forks are for." Amada smiles. "I thought the cake was for the wake."

"I did too."

"What happened?"

"My ex-sister-in-law didn't serve it. Says she forgot."

"Yep, I've heard that story before."

I stick the napkins and forks in my bag, pick up the coffees, and walk back to Cindy.

"The cashier says it's fine to serve the cake and that I can even announce it."

"This place is so accommodating," Cindy says as she begins cutting.

I knock on the table and with the projection of my teacher voice say, "We'd like to share our *tres leches* with you in honor of a hometown boy who had an untimely passing. If you'd like a piece, don't be shy." The room goes quiet, no noise from the machines, no chattering from the people. A hush that shows respect for our mortality. When I sit down, I notice a line forming.

Cindy gives everyone a generous serving, saving the two biggest for us.

I play with my cup, turning it in circles on the table while Cindy hosts. I need the movement, the constant rotation almost mesmerizing. If the cup were bigger or my hands smaller, I could lose myself totally in what looks like an abandoned well. All I'd have to do is dive in, hit my head hard against the bottom, and join Jacob on the other side.

"Ground control to Major Tom," Cindy sings off-key, repeating the lyric.

"You're such a smartass, Cindy."

"What's going on?" she asks.

"Jane told me Jacob shot himself." I tear up again, and Cindy digs a Kleenex from her purse.

"Shot himself?"

"That was the last thing she said to me before leaving the wake."

"Did you ask Susan?"

I nod, trying to block a vision of Jacob pooled in blood.

"And?"

"She denied it. Said Jane was trying to upset me."

"Why?"

"Because Nora blames me for ruining her marriage, and Jacob's kids hate me."

"Do you believe his kid or Susan?"

"I don't know. Susan grilled me on what Nora and I had talked about."

"That doesn't prove anything. She didn't want y'all speaking ill of the dear departed."

"Why a closed casket?" I ask.

"I'm glad it was closed," Cindy says. "I didn't want to see Jacob dead. Was he depressed?"

"He taught literature. He was a writer. And he didn't write about happy endings."

"I read some of his stuff. They're not going to make a *Lifetime* movie based on any of his stories."

I laugh loudly. Amada and her friends look over. Cindy puts her hand on mine and gives me another Kleenex.

"Did he ever talk about suicide?" she asks.

"We would discuss it in a grad student, drunk way. He thought it a human right."

"What?"

"Jacob thought Hemingway was a hero for taking charge of his own destiny."

"That's fucking sophomoric."

"I think so too."

"When did you last talk to him?"

"The night before the cleaning lady found him." I rub my neck, massaging the ache.

"How did he sound?" Cindy asks.

"Like Jacob. Always in regret. No published novel. No collection of stories."

"What else?"

"We talked about his moving back to Trion." I swirl my cup.

"I still wonder why you wanted him to return," she says.

"I wanted us to try again."

"He didn't want to be here."

"We'd have each other."

"Jacob would still be Jacob," Cindy says.

"Your point?" I ask.

"He never changed, and you're still blaming yourself for why things fell apart."

"I've always loved him and I'm tired of being alone, sleeping in an empty bed," I say.

"Get in line," she replies.

I want to scream at her. Why doesn't she understand?

"I've got to find out if he killed himself," I say.

"Ken would know. Ask him tomorrow," she says, folding her napkin into neat squares.

"I can't wait."

"What do you mean you can't wait?"

"I think I killed him."

"Bullshit."

"I told him we were done unless he moved back here."

"He was a grown man. He could say no."

"He couldn't write without me. I edited everything he wrote for the last ten years. He wouldn't submit a story unless I told him it was finished, even sent me cover letters to edit. About a year ago we argued about his coming down over spring break. He didn't, and I ghosted him more than a month. He finally called Susan and asked her to call me."

"That's sad. Regardless. You can't do anything tonight."

"I have to know."

"Then ask Nora," Cindy says.

"I don't know where she's staying."

"Only three motels in Trion," Cindy says.

"Let's go back to my place."

"Take him, William," Georgia said. "HE will protect you."
—Jacob Hall, "Behold, I Give You the Power"

# Chapter 21

The Williams House
Saturday, September 14, 2019
8:30 p.m.

Willy doesn't meet us at the door. I see my old Nikes, what I call yard sneakers, sprawled on the living room floor. One under the couch and the other by the Queen Anne. The laces are straggly and pulled partially out of the eyes. Willy's wedged behind the couch against the wall.

"What's the matter?" I ask.

Willy responds with a feeble thump of his tail while avoiding eye contact.

"Looks like Willy gave you a homecoming gift," Cindy yells from the kitchen.

When I walk in, I see poop at the backdoor. Not wet and messy, just a neat pile. But I scream, "Willy, why can't you use the litter box?" Grabbing a paper towel, I take the feces out to the garbage can before washing the spot.

"Here're the hotels and numbers," Cindy says, handing her iPhone to me. "Quality Inn, Royal Inn, and Econo Lodge."

With each hello, I ask, "May I speak to Nora Hall?" And with each call I get the same response: "There's no one registered by that name."

"Dead ends," I say and open the fridge for a Coca-Cola.

"Call Susan. Ask her where Nora is."

Thinking Susan won't tell me even if she knows, I figure that's another dead end though I call anyway,

"Hi, Susan. Do you know where Nora and the girls are staying?"

"Why do you want to know?"

"I need to ask Nora something."

"I told you they're just messing with you," she says.

"Please." I hope Susan's southern upbringing kicks in, making it impossible for her not to answer.

"Nora and the girls are taking a red eye out of Birmingham so they're probably spending the night there," Susan says.

"Which motel?"

"I have no idea."

"Thanks," I reply.

"What did she say?" Cindy asks.

"They're taking a red eye from Birmingham and are probably there."

"Most everybody stays at that Holiday Inn near the Birmingham Airport. Parking is free for a week," Cindy says, looking up the motel's phone number. She hands the iPhone to me.

"May I speak to Nora Hall?"

"Just one minute," the operator says.

"Hello."

"Nora?"

"Yes."

"This is Janet."

"What do you want?"

"Jane told me Jacob took his own life," I say, almost whispering.

"Leave us alone." The connection dies.

I listen to the beep, beep, beep, then all goes silent. "Go to hell, you fucking bitch."

"What did she say?" Cindy asks.

"Leave them alone."

"She sounds like a bitch to me," Cindy says.

"I'd probably say the same thing. Why should she help her ex-husband's other ex-wife?"

I lower my head on the table, hands cushioning, and feel the weight of Jacob's death. Believing he squandered his talent, he felt wasted for a long time. He left Trion at twenty, a kid with the potential of a forceful Southern voice, or so his teachers and professors predicted. And Jacob began to believe them until the burden of expectation became more than he could bear.

Willy sniffs my knees, buries his head in my lap. His face has a few white hairs around his eyes. If I take good care of him, he may live to be twelve or older. I know how to care for others, how to cater to their needs, watch for the signs. Will I eventually feel used and resent the time and attention spent on Willy? Will his puppy-like nature and licking and snuggling be enough to make up for the tethered responsibility I assume?

"Call Ken," Cindy says.

"Let's go over there."

"Where?"

"Ken's house. Harder to lie when you're looking someone in the face."

"You're right," she says. "I need to go to my car first."

She returns with a blue suitcase.

"Why do you have an overnight bag?"

"I keep it in the car in case I get lucky." She smiles.

"What?"

"Joke. I thought you might want the company tonight." She changes into jeans and a white hoodie while I put on jeans and a black USC sweatshirt.

"Glad to be free of the bra and heels," I say, hanging my outfit in the closet. I'm not much of a housekeeper these days; nevertheless, I can't stand clothes all over the floor and pile the dirties against the wall where Rhoda likes to sleep on my Uggs. I let Willy run around the back yard for five minutes before bringing him in.

"I'll drive," Cindy says. I reach in the fridge for two waters and leave on the kitchen light.

When we arrive at Ken's, his front porch is dark. We can see a glow from the side window. It's only 9:15, and most likely he's watching TV. If I'm the only one asking about Jacob, I think Ken will be more honest. Cindy stays in the car as I ring the front door bell. Seconds pass like minutes before the lights come on and the door opens.

"Janet?" Ken asks, his voice rising a notch or two.

"I need to ask you something," I say.

"What?"

"About Jacob's death."

"Jacob's death?"

"What was the cause?"

"I thought you knew," he says.

"I thought I knew too."

"What do you mean?"

"Susan said heart attack."

"So?"

"His daughter Jane said he shot himself."

Ken doesn't say a word. In his black shorts and gray T-shirt, he waits for me to say something else. Looking at him for the next words, I stand silent.

"And?" he asks.

"I want the truth."

"Janet, I can't discuss this with anybody except immediate family."

"I don't count?"

"Not an ex-wife. Wish I could help," he says.

"You can if you will." I know he knows the truth.

"And risk losing my license?"

"Come on, Ken. When do rules ever stop you?"

"Janet, I can't risk violation. You can't see the death records for twenty-five years."

Leaning in and lowering my voice, I say, "You should've thought of that earlier."

"What do you mean?"

"That one-nighter when Barbara was at a nursing Conference."

"You won't."

"I will if I need to." Trying hard not to blink, I look him dead on. My right calf feels tight, on the verge of cramping. Yet I don't move. I want Ken to sweat, to feel I will rat on him.

"We drank a lot that night, plus you came on to me."

"It's my fault you fucked me?"

He looks sad and somewhat older. His skin yellow in the dim light, his neck beginning to wobble like an old man's.

Holding her bathrobe together with both hands, Barbara walks toward him from behind. Her makeup is off and her hair's pulled back.

She comes to the door and hands Ken the phone. "You have a call from your answering service." Barbara looks at him then at me. "What's going on here?" A friend of Leann, Barbara is never pleasant, always snubbing me, even in high school, unless, of course, Jacob was around. Barbara has a Miss Piggy appearance and air that become more striking with age and money.

"Janet has a question I can't answer," Ken says. "Sorry. Good night. I need to take this call."

He walks back down the hall, and Barbara closes the door without acknowledging me.

All I have to do is ring the bell again and call him out to his wife. I'll describe how he fucked me in the king bed that is their twenty-fifth anniversary gift to each other. How Ken and I stained her clean flamingo sheets.

The guitarist stopped playing and the organ died out. The congregation quieted. Uncle John stood behind Georgia, his snake back in the box. My hands turned palms up and my arms began to float, then the rattler turned its cruel eyes on me.

—Jacob Hall, "Behold, I Give You the Power"

# Chapter 22

The Williams House
Saturday, September 14, 2019
9:30 p.m.

I hear Willy pawing the door before I turn the key. Rhoda, of course, is nowhere in sight, probably still in the closet.

"It's nine thirty and Jim Beam time." I pour myself a bourbon and Coke, thinking the fizz will be good for my stomach. "Want one, Cindy?"

"Sure," she says, dropping into the kitchen chair.

"What am I going to do?"

"Let it go."

"I can't. I tipped him over the edge." I want to hide, mostly from myself, and slide the rest of the Coke back into the fridge above a carton of eggs and a Krispy Kreme box several days old that emits a stale cold smell.

"Why are you blaming yourself?" Cindy asks.

"How can I not? Jacob said our divorce almost killed him."

"That was then. Wasn't he sleeping with Nora?"

"And I slept with Ana." I hear Cindy's toe tapping the table leg. She never sits without crossing her legs and swinging the top one back and forth, a metronome marking an exact beat. I feel time is passing without me. I feel abandoned, stranded in some unfamiliar place with nothing to ground me except sad memories.

"After the divorce he called every day, his voice broken, begging me to come back."

"You didn't," Cindy says.

"We had sex, and I spent hours reading and editing his work." I remember those nights. He'd fall into a deep sleep, snoring, and I'd retreat to the kitchen, make coffee, and edit his latest short story.

"You never mentioned that," Cindy says.

I've never been totally honest about my past with Jacob and feel he's my burden to bear. I can't live with him. I can barely live without him. During those days after the divorce, our roles flipped. He was the one in greater need, the one who had to be weaned. And I was there until he was ready to let go. Those were what I called our marriage-a-trois years. I slept occasionally with Ana and often with Jacob. He slept with Nora and me. I never talked about him with Ana, and I doubt he ever mentioned me to Nora. Then he married her and moved eight hundred miles away. But he never let go. Neither did I. There was a kind of thrill for us in our post-marriage relationship, existing together in the shadows.

"We need a plan, Cindy. I can't go to bed not knowing."

"Let's dig up the grave," Cindy says.

"What?"

"You want to find out."

Rubbing my face, I can't believe what I'm hearing. Dig up Jacob's grave? I look down at Willy, eyes shut and peacefully asleep, his snore hardly audible.

"Are you serious?" I ask.

"How else are you going to find out?"

"It feels wrong. Disturbing the dead."

"He's gone. That's a corpse."

"I know, I know."

"Don't you want to find out?"

"Body snatching? We could be arrested."

"Who in Trion would arrest you?"

"The thought of digging up Jacob creeps me out."

"Then let it go," Cindy replies.

"I have to know."

I envision Jacob after I hang up on him. Phone in his hand. Signal gone. Willy asleep. Next to the manuscript on Jacob's desk, a bottle of bourbon. His clothesline empty of pages because a publisher rejected his novel. Maybe the gun alongside the bottle. Just in case. My threat, which in his mind would doom his writing, is the inciting incident. To cover the taste of the barrel, he takes one more long pull on the bottle.

"Okay. Let's dig him up," I say.

"They keep the coffin key inside the coffin," Cindy says.

"How do you know?"

"Just watched 'How to Open a Casket' on YouTube."

"Are we going to break into the funeral home?" I ask.

"No. Ken's there now. Remember the call."

"So?"

"You're going to distract him while I steal a key," Cindy says.

"Then go to the cemetery and dig up Jacob?"

"Exactly," she says. "How many shovels do you have?"

I grab my flashlight, and we go to the garage. I pull the light cord turning on a 120-watt bulb, illuminating the inside like a full moon. Three shovels, two with wooden handles and the other with a metal handle, lean against the back wall beside jelly jars full of used nails, some rusty, some shiny.

"Aunt Grace was quite the gardener." I pull out several pairs of heavy cotton gloves from the utility box. Looking for the snuggest fit, Cindy and I try them on.

"Shovels, gloves, flashlight. What else do we need?"

"Jim Beam," Cindy says. "I have another flashlight in my Honda."

"I'll get the bourbon and lock the house."

We put the shovels in the back of her Accord and tumble into the front seat. The air's drier and cooler than usual for an early September night. I like the coolness, knowing it cuts down on mosquitoes.

"When we get to the funeral home, you know the routine," she says.

"Roger. As I pull off the damsel in distress to distract Ken, you steal a matching coffin key."

Moseley Funeral Home is a beacon on George Wallace Drive. The front's locked. Pinching my cheeks so they look red and bothered while Cindy smokes a cigarette next to the car, I ring the bell. In his khakis and white golf shirt, Ken opens the door. I rush past him to his office and start riffling through the papers on his desk.

"Stop that," he hollers as he enters the room.

"I need to know about Jacob. I was his wife."

"Thirty-five years ago. You have no standing, no rights," he says and pulls me away from the desk.

"How can you be such a bastard?"

"Janet, please. Calm down."

Plopping into a brown leather chair cushioned to soothe the ailing bones of the living, I stare at the walls covered with certificates and diplomas from businesses that deal with funeral rites: embalming, cremation, burial plots, gravestones. Ken sits behind his desk, appropriately appointed with an Olan Mills portrait of Barbara and him, she sitting and he standing beside her, his hand on her shoulder. Both dressed in blue, his blue suit with a red bowtie and her navy cotton dress with a white lace collar and deep decolletage. Then a family shot of them sitting on a sofa with their two daughters.

"If I tell you anything confidential, I'll lose my license."

"I won't tell on you."

"Really?"

"I never told Barbara about our one-nighter."

"You can't tell her now either."

"Why not? If you don't help me, why should I help you?" I mean it. I would do almost anything to find out whether Jacob shot himself.

"'Cause you're decent," he says. "It will ruin my family." Glaring at me like a male Medusa, Ken's unflinching, his eyes like drill holes where the living become gray dust.

"What about me?" I ask. "Carrying the weight of Jacob's suicide."

"You?"

"I talked to him the night before his body was found. I pushed him over the edge."

"What did you say?"

Shaking my head, I start to cry. I intend the tears to prolong my stay in his office, giving Cindy enough time to find the key. However, my tears are real. An expert in soothing the bereaved, Ken comes to me, hands me some tissues, and pulls a chair close.

"I've seen lots of bodies and lots of suicides. It's never the fault of the person left. Otherwise, it's called murder."

"What do you mean by murder, Ken?"

"I mean it's been a long day and you're blaming yourself for nothing."

"Because he didn't kill himself?" I ask, eager to extract some information.

"I didn't say that. It's late, you're tired."

I know Ken will never risk losing his job, though losing his wife is another issue. Our tryst was probably not his first. With a relaxed manner, calm and deft, he took me back to his house for the night. A first-timer would be nervous and clumsy.

I spot Cindy walking toward his office.

"Hey, girl, let's go home," she says, her right thumb raised.

At the door I tell Ken, "You're on borrowed time.

I heard a hiss and knew that snake would kill me because I didn't believe in God. And even if I did, I didn't believe in my ability to accept the Holy Ghost into me, for I was, and still am, a jaded academic whose life would lose its meaning if God existed.

—Jacob Hall, "Behold, I Give You the Power"

# Chapter 23

Jackson Memorial Cemetery
Saturday, September 14, 2019
10:15 p.m.

Cindy and I arrive at Jacob's grave, cut off the engine, and sit in the dark car. Taking a swig of Jim Beam, I pass the bottle to Cindy.

"What in the hell are we doing?" she asks.

"Waiting 'til our gut says start."

"We could be charged with a crime," she says. "Are you ready to spend the night in jail?"

"Who's going to arrest us in Trion? Those are your very words," I reply.

"Any cruising cop, bored and driving through a heap of dead bodies."

"We know most of those boys in blue."

"You think they'd ignore a couple of body snatchers?"

"You seemed to think so earlier. Anyway, we're not going to snatch him. I just want to see him. I have to know or ...."

"Or what?" Cindy asks. "You'll kill yourself?"

"I can't say that 'Do not go gentle into that good night' hasn't floated across my mind."

I roll down the window and stick out my hand, hoping to find fall somewhere in the air. The distant sound of an eighteen-wheeler, shifting gears to climb the mountain, breaks the stillness.

"I have to know."

Cindy studies me then says, "Let's go."

Jacob's grave doesn't look like what I expected: a mound of extra dirt heaped over the top to compress in time so that grass can be planted. Instead, a section of artificial turf covers his grave and gives the appearance of a lush green lawn. Already in place is a black marble headstone that I didn't even notice earlier, unable to turn away from the coffin during the burial.

We roll up the turf, and Cindy bends over to feel the soil. "It's not too hard," she says, and I groan. Cindy's handier with tools and yard equipment than I am. The closest I come to digging and hoeing is snipping off deadheads of roses and azaleas, behavior I tease myself into thinking is yard work, clipping the bushes close so the new buds have room and resources to blossom. Watching them evolve into full flower brings me a certain kind of joy, a certain pleasure that digging in the soil doesn't. Dirt under my nails or debris from inside the gardening gloves annoys me, and I don't understand how working one's fingers in wormy loam brings gratification.

But tonight is different. The earth is already less compressed where they dug Jacob's plot not even eight hours earlier. The moon is full, shedding plenty of light. Regardless of other obstacles, with the obvious being my age and all the alcohol I've consumed, I want to try. I've come too far not to.

"How you doing?" Cindy asks.

"Not bad."

"Good workout," she says.

"Rather be at the gym, spinning or walking on a treadmill. People are animated there."

"How're your hands?"

"These gloves are okay."

"I can't believe we're doing this," Cindy says.

"Glad the soil's cooperating. I'd never be able to dig up hard ground."

"My back is killing me," she says, massaging the small of her back with the heel of her hand.

The fall crickets' loud chirps provide background for the occasional car. Nevertheless, I hear something different, more like twigs snapping and leaves crunching.

"Evening, ladies."

"Shit," Cindy screams and turns to see the local drunk, Homer Lee. "What the fuck?" she asks.

"I sleep here some nights. Quiet place with soft grass. Nobody bothers me," he says.

Drinking and doing drugs before most of us, he was a grade behind me. His uncle, may he rest in peace, was a bass guitar player with a negative influence on his nephew. He wears an AC/DC T-shirt and jeans with Doc Martins.

"Did Betty Jean kick you out again?" I ask.

"Yep, calls me a nuisance."

"What did you do this time?" Cindy asks.

"I might have puked on her coffee table. It's a bit hazy."

"That's enough to ask you to leave," I say, taking a sip of the bourbon.

Looking at the shovels and pile of dirt, he asks, "What are y'all up to?"

"We're digging up a grave," Cindy says.

"Why?"

"Want to find things out," I reply.

"What things?"

"None of your business," I say.

"Then I'll make it my business."

"What do you mean?" Cindy asks.

"I'll ask the caretaker."

"Don't do that, Homer," I say.

"Maybe I won't, maybe I will. Depending," he says, sticking his hands in his pockets and eyeing the Jim Beam.

"Depending on what?"

"Whether or not you give me that bottle."

"And if I do?" I say.

"I don't see a thing. I'll go back to my plot and sleep."

"It's all yours. If word gets out about us being here, I'm calling the cops and reporting you for vandalism," Cindy says without dropping a beat and hands him the bottle.

"I hear you. Whose grave?"

We look at each other. I shrug.

"Jacob Hall's."

"Weren't you married to him?" Homer asks me.

"I was. We divorced."

"Sorry to hear he's gone. Sorry y'all didn't make it."

"Thanks. I appreciate that."

He sits on the ground with the bottle between his legs. "Want a nip?"

"I'm fine," Cindy says.

I shake my head no.

Looking blissful, he takes a drink. "How long you been at it?" he asks.

"An hour," Cindy says.

Homer frowns but doesn't say what we all think, that Cindy and I aren't up to this digging.

"This isn't the first time I see someone messing with a grave at night. Must've been six years ago. These young fellas were digging up old Mr. Abernathy's grave. You remember him. Richest man in town. Biggest house on Millionaire Mile. Owned four car dealerships."

"Did you get a bottle from them?" I ask.

"Hell no. They would of cracked my skull with a shovel and thrown me in the hole."

"Who were they?" Cindy asks.

"Hell if I know. One had on a sailor's hat, and the other was bare headed. Definitely not female."

"Why not?" I ask.

He grins. "Well, I never guessed no ladies to be grave robbers 'til now."

"We're not."

"No offense. Anyway, old Abernathy wore enough gold to buy someone a good used car. I guess them boys thought they buried him with his rings, chains, and cufflinks."

"What did you do?" Janet asked.

"I walked away real quiet and at a distance yelled, 'What the fuck's going on?'"

Cindy and I laugh.

"Well done, Homer," Cindy says.

"You're not going to do anything unnatural, are you?"

"No," I say. "I just want to see Jacob one last time."

"It was a closed casket," Cindy says.

Taking another drink, Homer watches us. "Y'all have always been nice to me. I believe you," he says.

"Want to lend a hand?" I ask.

"I wouldn't feel right," he says. He takes a bow and turns in a haphazard fashion that displays a man who's learned to navigate his world with as much dignity as his choices allow.

"Good night, ladies, and thanks for the bourbon."

Cindy pulls out a cigarette. Before she lights it, I ask for one. The Bic's flame ruins my night vision. When it returns, our glowing cigarette tips remind me of fireflies poking holes in the night.

"I wish there were fireflies," I say.

"Do you remember Pogo Possum?" she asks.

"Sure. I didn't understand much of what was going on until I was older. It was the Doonesbury of its time."

"There's one about fireflies," she says. "Pogo talks to a firefly and asks him why he flashes on and off. 'Women,' the firefly says. Pogo doesn't understand, and the firefly explains, 'When we flash on, we spot them. When we flash off, we sneak up on them.'"

I laugh, then quit, realizing the joke's misogyny. We're quiet and smoking, listening for cars or some other graveyard camper to appear.

I drop my cigarette and crush it. "That's not funny anymore."

"I know. It was true back then, and I kind of miss the attention," Cindy says.

Scanning the grave, I realize that our effort has achieved no more than a foot dug. Cindy looks tired, and I'm about to fall over.

"Why don't we take turns digging from the headstone down. When we hit—"

"If we hit …," Cindy interrupts.

"When," I repeat, "we hit the coffin, we can go on from there. I'll dig first," I offer with the "if" fluctuating.

Georgia moved closer and raised the snake higher. Its split tongue flicked out and I ran—out the door, through the parking lot, down the road. I ran toward the safety of my books and my classroom. I ran as long as my smoke-compromised lungs would allow. When I stopped, I bent over, falling to my knees, and surrendered the Coke and egg sandwich. The sharp gravel cut into my palms.

—Jacob Hall, "Behold, I Give You the Power"

# Chapter 24

Jackson Memorial Cemetery
Saturday, September 14, 2019
10:45 p.m.

My phone rings, and I pull it out of my side pocket.
"Ken's calling."
"Probably suspects we're up to something," Cindy says.
I mute the ringer.
"I slept with him once," she says.
"Ken?"
"No. Jacob."
I stop digging, squeeze the handle with both hands until I feel my skin chafing.
"When?"
"One Friday night after a game. My parents were out of town, and I was supposed to spend the night with a friend."
"Why did you lie about it earlier?"
"You seemed pissed enough about Leann."
While I remain standing, the shovel still in my hand, she sits on the ground. With my left hand I motion for her to keep talking.
"He wasn't my first. Like you, I started early," she says.
I begin to shovel again, emptying Jacob's grave, my hands almost numb.
"Details," I say.
"Sorry I mentioned it."
"Tell me, Cindy."
"We did it in his truck on a quilt his grandmother made."
"By the live oak?" I ask.

"Magnolia tree, I think. A bunch of mosquitos bit my ass."

Thinking how those bites must've itched, I feel my scowl slide into a smirk.

"Just once?"

"Just once. After Jacob got a steady girl, my sleeping with him didn't feel right."

"A girlfriend didn't stop him," I reply.

"Did me."

"He must've been good since you remember details."

"Yep," she says.

"He was the best I ever had," I reply, the dirt more packed with each shovelful.

"What about Ana?"

"I should've qualified. Best guy lover."

"Was Jacob jealous?"

Recalling his reticence about Ana, I lean on the shovel, thankful for a respite.

"Several weeks after I lost him to Nora at Dr. Greinor's party, Jacob and I were lying together sweaty after sex. He asked if Ana was as good."

"What did you say?" Cindy asks.

"I said he was the best ever."

"Was he?"

"He almost always came before I did. Ana made sure we came together. Sometimes foreplay with her lasted hours. Every place on our bodies was a playground. But she wasn't Jacob."

"What do you mean?"

"When Jacob was inside me, I felt whole. Never wanted him to come out."

"Bad timing for Jacob's question," Cindy says.

"I thought so too. The questioning was part of his insecurity."

"How long was your relationship with Ana?" Cindy asks.

"Off and on, we were sexually involved one year before the divorce and two years after."

"Did you live together?"

"No. I wanted my own space. We were good friends and good fuck buddies. Still I didn't want another relationship. I wanted to be with myself."

"What happened to her?"

"She got a Ph.D. in English and a tenure-track job at Reed College. She met a woman there, and they've been together more than twenty years."

"Do you stay in touch?"

"We exchange the occasional email as our lives have grown in different directions. She knows I've always had a sweet spot for Jacob. Have you ever slept with a woman?"

"I was a theater major." Cindy smiles.

Hearing the muffled engine of a car roll through the cemetery, I sit down beside the grave. Raising my butt slightly off the hard earth, I lean to the front and look at Cindy, a faint, shadowy trace in the night.

"Jacob always seemed so confident in high school. When he spoke, it was like that EF Hutton ad," Cindy says. "Everybody listened."

"When I was fifteen, he was the smartest, most talented guy I'd ever met," I reply.

"What happened to him?"

"Life. Age," I say.

"That happens to us all."

"He was burdened by expectations."

"What?" Cindy asks. "And we weren't?"

"Only our own. Nobody expected much of us. Good little girls who'd be good little wives."

"Jacob was a male," Cindy says.

"You got it. And he had potential. His teachers thought so, his peers, me. Especially me."

"He was a grown man."

"I know. When he was young, he felt compelled to write. Every day since high school, he'd write a sketch or poem or bit of a story. I read them all, at first."

"Why you? He was the writer," Cindy asks.

"I was his girl. He wanted me to like it. As time went on, I studied lit and became a better reader. He wanted to impress me more than before. Nora said he wrote for me. I was the ideal reader in his head."

"That's a lot of pressure on you."

"That's why I feel responsible for his death."

"Jacob could be a pompous ass at times," Cindy says. "What about your wedding dinner at the Holiday Inn?"

"He had way too much bourbon."

"He rose to toast you and finished thirty minutes later. Everybody rolled their eyes."

"Mike says Jacob had to be reminded every so often that he came from Trion, Alabama."

"Why do you think things would have been different now?"

"Because I'd be the one in control. The power shifted. He depended on my approval. Without it, he was consumed by his own sense of failure."

"Are men that fragile?" she asks.

"Everybody is in one way or another. Why are you so negative about Jacob?"

"He was a fucking loser of a dad and a shit husband."

"Cindy, I love you dearly for helping me dig him up. No matter what you say, I'm going to feel guilty."

Except for the occasional low whir of a passing car or the trill of a mockingbird, the night is still. I feel Cindy's disapproval.

"Did Jacob even have a gun?"

"His dad's guns, a shotgun and a pistol."

"Did he hunt?"

"He did as a kid. You know how everybody around here hunts. When we were in South Carolina, Roger Buckelew took him duck hunting once."

"How many did Jacob shoot?" Cindy asks.

"Didn't even pull the trigger."

"Why not?"

"He said they were too beautiful to kill, flying across the lake in a yellow and orange sunrise, their bodies art in flight."

"How could a man like that shoot himself?" she asks.

"Hemingway shot himself," I say.

"But he was a macho kind of guy."

"Jacob was still a boy from Trion. And he was a writer. He could construct a story that made whatever he did seem heroic."

"Jacob wasn't a boy," she says.

"Wasn't he? All those guys we saw today are just older versions of their high school selves. They never left Trion. Even if they left physically, like Jacob, they are still part of the good-ole-Trion-boys circle."

"But Jacob wanted to be a dad," Cindy says.

"Thought he was supposed to have kids. That's what a man does," I reply.

"Sperm blame is something we did in the 70s," she says.

"And it still holds true. Many guys who want kids don't want to sacrifice other desires for those of offspring. He left his girls to Nora just like Leann's husband left their three kids to her."

"That's why I never wanted a husband," Cindy says.

"You were smart to raise your kid by yourself.

My right arm begins to hurt. "Your turn," I say, sitting in front of the dirt. Feeling my phone vibrate, I figure it's Ken and don't bother to check who's calling. I drink some water and pass the bottle to Cindy, the moon almost sitting on her shoulders.

"Is Mike one of those good ole Trion boys?" she asks.

"I think he's the showroom model."

"Is he like your dad?"

"No. Mike is a kind guy."

"What do you mean?"

"My dad was tough to live with," I say. "He slapped me if he didn't like what I said. That heavy right hand would come flying across my face."

"Did your mother know?"

"She saw it."

"What did she do?"

"Nothing. Absolutely nothing. He slapped me until I was fifteen, his knuckles often leaving faint bruises. The last time I remember was one Saturday afternoon at home when their friends came to cook out. He hit me in front of them. I don't recall what I'd said."

"What happened then?"

"I stalked off. As long as he lived, if he moved suddenly and I was near him, I'd flinch. The body memory never leaves."

"Did you tell Jacob?"

"Of course. He said he'd kill him if he ever hit me again. After I started dating Jacob, my father kept his hands to himself."

"Did he hit your mom?"

"Not that I ever saw, though she had a lot of black and blue spots on her skin that seemed to appear from nowhere."

"Did you ask her?"

"Mother just said her skin was thin and not to worry."

"Did you ever talk to him about it?"

"When he was in his 80s, I asked him why he slapped me."

"And?"

"He denied it. Said he never laid a hand on me. That I was hallucinating from smoking too much pot. I reminded him of spanking me with his leather belt."

"Did he deny that?"

"No. He said, and I quote, 'You turned out good because of it.'"

"No wonder you didn't like him," Cindy says. "It's funny I wound up having a boy. Always wanted a girl but figured Tommy was my chance to raise a boy like I wanted him to be. Kind and gentle."

"You always want a kid?" I ask.

"Being an only child, I wanted a sibling and decided early that a child was the closest to a brother or sister I'd get. I've never regretted the decision."

"What did your folks say?"

"It was my choice. I was twenty-three and had finished my first year of little theater in Atlanta. I planned on being a single mom."

"They sound great."

"Dad wasn't rough or violent. He grew up in a Baptist preacher's family," she says.

"From what I've heard, that doesn't mean much. Remember Brother Jones at Mount Calvary Baptist. His son was the biggest pothead in town and what a slut."

"You're right. Except Dad came from a staunch country preacher who believed in disciplining his kids with the stink eye and silence."

"Your own dad the same way?"

"Pretty much. Mom mostly raised me, yet he was there if I needed him."

"Did you?"

"Did I what?" she asks.

"Need him."

"Not much," she says.

"Mike was my stand-in dad. I wanted to play baseball, so he spent hours playing catch with me, and he didn't even like the game. He was such a sweet brother. He pitched 'til my arm wore out from swinging. Then we switched."

"Where'd you play? No girl teams were here back then."

"I'd play in neighborhood pick-up games or at school. No boy could swing a bat stronger than I could. Almost batted five hundred or better every time." I feel my phone vibrate again and trust Ken will give up after three tries.

"Do you think I'm anywhere close to the coffin?" Cindy asks.

"Shouldn't be much farther," I say, my shoulder still aching.

"At least we're not covered in mosquitos," she says.

"Jacob and I married in September."

"Why this month?"

"Superstition. I'm a Virgo. Mother always said if nuptial and natal dates match, good luck follows. We married on my birthday, September fifteenth."

"What do you think happened?" Cindy asks.

"Our luck ran out."

Clunk. Her shovel hits a hard surface.

"I think I struck the coffin," Cindy says and pushes the dirt away. The surface is rough.

I turn on the flashlight and beam it on her hand on the coffin. It's dark gray, not shiny like metal.

"That looks like cement," she says.

"Cement?" I reply, staring down. "That makes no sense."

I pull my phone out and type in *casket, cement*. I have only one bar and hand the phone to Cindy. "See if you can get a better signal."

She walks around, pauses, and then reads aloud from the phone.

"Burial vault, a container made to enclose a coffin. Previously made of wood and now made of cement to help prevent a grave from sinking."

I hold the flashlight on Cindy. She walks back to the grave, sits down, and dangles her legs over the cement.

"We're fucked," I say and sit next to her.

"Yes, we are."

Stomping on the cement, I shout, "Damn it, Jacob. Why in the hell did you do this?"

My right leg tingles from the impact, and I want to kick Jacob for acting like a selfish brat.

"I wish we'd kept that bottle," Cindy says.

How long I knelt there, I don't remember.

—Jacob Hall, "Behold, I Give You the Power"

# Chapter 25

Jackson Memorial Cemetery
Saturday, September 14, 2019
11:15 p.m.

Red and white car lights flash in our direction. I switch off the flashlight. A car pulls up, and a spotlight shines on the pile of dirt next to the grave. A door opens and I hear footsteps approach.

"Stand up with your hands in the air."

We comply. Two flashlights shine on us as the red and white flashes cycle through the surrounding graves and sparse trees.

"Cindy, is that you?"

"Sam?" she asks.

"What the hell are you up to?" her cousin's son asks and turns off his flashlight.

"I want to see Jacob," I say.

The other cop, Randy, who let me off with a warning for rolling through a stop sign about a month before, lowers his light. A mismatched pair, Sam's slim and tall, maybe six-two, whereas Randy's about a head shorter with a round belly.

"We're just digging up Jacob's grave," Cindy says.

"It's against the law for any citizen without due cause to dig up a body," Randy announces.

I imagine how freaky we must look, two women old enough to be their mothers, sitting on a burial vault in a freshly unearthed grave.

"We're not trying to break any laws," I say. "I just need to see Jacob's body."

"You'd need some block and tackle to get the cement case off the coffin," Sam says.

"We found out the hard way," Cindy replies.

Sam offers his hand and pulls Cindy out of the grave. Randy offers his hand to me, and I accept.

"Ladies, we're just going to pretend this event never happened," Sam says. "We'll shovel the dirt back in."

"We can't ignore this, Sam," Randy says.

"I'm the senior officer here," Sam replies.

"They're breaking the law."

"Have some heart. She's just lost her ex-husband."

"If he's an ex, why does she want to see him again anyway?"

"Ask her, Randy," Sam says.

"It's personal," my voice cracks.

"Why did you divorce him if you want to see him so much?" Randy asks.

"That's personal too."

Randy pulls out his phone.

"You get a stronger signal over there," Cindy says and points to a headstone about ten feet away.

Randy walks over and fiddles with his phone. "Ladies, you have violated Alabama Code Title 13A." Randy pauses and adds, "Willfully desecrating a grave."

"What's wrong with you, boy?" Sam asks. "I'm not going to charge these ladies."

"Then I'll have to report you, too, Sam," Randy says, shining his flashlight on Sam.

"Get that thing off me," Sam shouts.

Randy lowers the light again.

"You go ahead and arrest these ladies. When we leave here, we're going to stop by Nancy's house on the way to the station."

"Nancy who?" I ask.

"Nancy Phillips, Randy's aunt. I'm going to knock on her door, and when she answers, I'll smell the joint she's just put out. With probable cause I'll search her home and you damn well know she has enough weed in there to be charged with possession with intent to sell. And we can carry all three ladies to the station."

"Nancy has glaucoma," Randy says.

"I know," Sam replies. "That's why I've never knocked on her door."

"Now, y'all sit there while Randy and I shovel this dirt back in."

"I ain't shoveling shit," Randy says and walks back to the cruiser.

Sam starts to shovel when Randy turns the flashers and spotlight off.

Cindy uses her flashlight to guide Sam.

I walk over to the police cruiser. "I'm sorry, Randy."

"Wish I'd given you a ticket."

I laugh and he tries not to smile. Randy's a man who should never lie to his girlfriend.

Watching Sam move the earth back, we lean against the car.

"Why are you doing this?" he asks.

"I think Jacob shot himself, and it was my fault."

"I heard he had a heart attack."

"I heard different, and I have to know."

Before talking, Randy looks down at his feet for a couple of minutes. "When I was a rookie and partnered with Ed Landers who retired to Gulf Shores, we were involved in a shooting at the 7-Eleven by Hardee's. As we pulled up, two perps came out of the store, and one started to fire at us. Taking cover behind the car, we returned fire and killed a fourteen-year-old boy that day."

"I'm so sorry."

"They couldn't determine whose gun killed him. The bullets were damaged and, to be honest, I don't think it mattered enough to the people in the lab to figure it out."

I touch Randy's arm, and he turns toward me.

"It's not going to make a damn bit of difference. Regardless of whether you're responsible, Jacob's death will haunt you. For well into three years, not a day passes that I don't see that kid lying on the pavement and bleeding next to an oil stain the shape of Florida," Randy says. "I'm going to help Sam finish. He's probably sweated enough to stink up the car."

I slide to the ground and bury my face in my hands. After a while, I look up and the other three are standing in front of me.

"Cindy, are you able to drive?" Sam asks.

"Sure. Don't tell Loretta about this."

"I don't think there's much you can do that would surprise my mama. We'll follow you back," Sam says, handing us the shovels.

Finally, I stood—panting, drenched by sweat, blood dripping off my palms, and surrounded by the green landscape that accepted my presence. Birds sang and insects began to seek me out. I was on a two-lane road with no signs or markers in view. No distinguishing features. I could be in Ohio or Pennsylvania. Even the litter offered no clue. This place could be Purgatory, and I could be dead from a snake bite on the floor of the Red Rock Holiness Church. My head in Georgia's lap. Uncle John and the congregation holding hands and praying for my soul. The tall man playing some obscure hymn on his SG while the organist looked on.

—Jacob Hall, "Behold, I Give You the Power"

# Chapter 26

The Williams House
Saturday, September 14, 2019
11:45 p.m.

When we walk through the front door, Willy's waiting for us, jumping up and down. I reach down, pet him, and let him out. We watch him sniff out a suitable place to pee then trot back in, tail wagging.

"We're happy to be here too, Willy," I say and go into the kitchen.

"Near the Witching Hour. I ought to be going home," Cindy says.

"What about a nightcap?"

"Make it a Coke," she says.

I pop the caps off two bottles of Coca-Cola.

"Do you want to get high?" I ask and dig the joint out of my pocket. It's somewhat crushed and bent though still serviceable.

"Where did you get that?"

"At the gettin' place."

"I'm glad Sam and Randy didn't search us."

Lighting it, I take a drag. Having already been polluted by one of Cindy's cigarettes, my lungs accept the smoke without complaint. Cindy takes a hit and holds the smoke before letting it go.

"Look at these blisters." Exposing two fluid-filled bubbles on each hand, I hold up my palms.

"What do you expect? I can match you," Cindy says and opens her palms.

"I haven't smoked pot since the MLA conference with Jacob."

"Plenty of the folks in Atlanta smoke, but I haven't in Trion. Did you smoke in high school?"

"No. First in college."

I feel calmer and rather dissociated. Maybe I should meet Randy's Aunt Nancy.

"I'm pretty fucked up," Cindy says.

Sharing the joint at the kitchen table, we turn quiet. The occasional thump of Willie's tail is the only sound I hear while Cindy absentmindedly pets him. I wish we'd saved some cake and start thinking about what's in the fridge. "American Pie" begins to play in my head—"the day the music died."

"I still don't know what happened to Jacob."

Cindy kneels next to my chair and wraps her arms around me. I cry.

"What's it going to change?" she asks. "He's gone. Either he died of natural causes or he didn't. You're not responsible either way."

"I threatened him," I say.

"He was a grown man."

"Until now, I didn't know what it was to have my heart broken."

"Losing anybody is hard, especially when it's your first love, and maybe the love of your life," she says. "You're feeling survivor's guilt. You're here. He's not."

She lets me go. I push back the chair wondering if he's somewhere near, listening to our conversation.

"Do you want me to stay?"

"Willy and Rhoda will take care of me."

Cindy fetches her suitcase from the bedroom, and we walk back to the front. I hug her like Aunt Grace used to hug me, squeezing all the air out.

"Call me tomorrow," she says and gets into her Honda.

Lingering at the door, I watch the car until it turns on Pecan Avenue. When I go back in, I drop my clothes by the washer in the kitchen and head to the shower. I want the smell of Jacob's grave off my skin, out of my hair. The shower takes forever. The water's unable to cleanse as I lather and scrub over and over. My skin feels like a hair shirt I've worn for days, chafing my body, telling me that living is the greater pain. I turn the shower on hot and watch the steam cover the room in clouds, hiding the mirror and sink, toilet, and walls in a fog.

I could faint in such heat, hit my head on the tile, and never wake up. Cindy or Mike would find my shriveled carcass and assume guilt for my passing, never knowing whether it was an accident or willful intent—the abandoned lover seeking to be with her love in the next world. The perfect ending of a Brontë novel, the retelling of Catherine and Heathcliff's narrative. Yet I'm not isolated. I have Rhoda and now Willy, Jacob's impish gift, to watch over. Yes, I have them to care for, parting trick or not.

In the shower, I turn my back to the nozzle before raising my head for the water to cascade over my neck and shoulders, finally washing away the day. The grit from the graveyard slides down and swirls at my feet as the hot water turns temperate then cool. Wrapping myself in a terrycloth beach towel, I feel worn down by grief, not sure I can ever shake this feeling. Does it matter if he died by his own hand or by natural causes? The truth is that he's gone, never again to stride through my door. I'm not one to carry the burden of the past, though today I feel the weight I've ignored, reaching for the handles to turn off the baptismal font. I dry myself, hang the towel over the shower rod, and walk into my bedroom, leaving wet prints behind.

From the end of the bed, I stare at Rhoda, snuggled between the pillows, and reach for my garnet USC nightshirt. Not the original from grad school, one I bought before moving back. No matter the time of year, I like to sleep in a nightshirt and cotton pajama bottoms. The house is quiet, Willy asleep in the corner. My bones are weary, tired of the day's sadness, and my head is numb from the pot when I hear tap, tap, tap at the front.

I grab my flannel bathrobe, guessing the knock is Ken's. I can't imagine he makes a habit of consoling widows with a house call, and he's too well-intended to show up for a quickie though he probably wants one. He's called three times, and I haven't picked up. Most likely he's pissed and wants to know why Cindy and I came to the funeral home.

After checking through the peephole, I open the door.

"Did Jacob shoot himself?" I ask, my hand wrapped around the door handle.

"You know I can't tell you that."

"Then why are you here?"

"Why didn't you answer my calls?"

"My phone was turned off."

"I was worried about you," he says.

"I'm okay."

"Can I come in?" His voice brittle and croaky from the long day.

"I'm not dressed for company."

"You're fine," he says, patting my back. "I won't stay long."

"Want something to drink?" I ask as he follows me to the kitchen.

"What are you offering?"

"Coke, beer, bourbon. Your choice."

"I'll take a beer even if I'm on the clock."

I open the fridge and pull out two Millers, find an unopened package of Oreos, and hand a beer to Ken who twists the cap off and gives it back to me. I smile and hand him the unopened beer.

"You know I've twisted open my fair share of beers," I say.

"Sorry. Old habit," he says. "Oreos and beer?"

"Have you been at the funeral home all this time?" I ask, twisting the cookie apart and  scraping the filling with my teeth before eating the cookie.

"Saturday night can get busy," he replies.

Sitting across from me at the table, he leans on his elbows. Trying to wash away that dry scratchiness from the dirt, I take a long swallow.

"Do you always work Saturday?" I ask.

"More people die on this day than any other."

"Why?" I ask and deconstruct another Oreo.

"Car accidents, gun shots, and drug overdoses," he says. "Heart attacks still kill most people. Nearly twice the other causes."

"I wouldn't want your job." I rub the bottle, my fingers alive to the cold.

"Good money. Somebody's always dying," he says.

"Morbid way to spend your time," I say.

"You get used to it." He takes an Oreo, inspects it, and pops the whole thing in his mouth.

"If you like living in a Stephen King novel," I roll my eyes and recall being traumatized for weeks after reading *Pet Sematary*.

"You don't seem the Stephen King type," he says.

"While I'm not anymore, he's not a bad writer. Knows how to tell a story."

"What do you mean?" Ken asks. "I don't read many books myself. Mainly newspapers and magazines."

"He knows how to keep your interest and build a plot."

"Is that the kind of stuff Jacob wrote?"

"No. He was more of a word man."

"Meaning?"

"Language came before story."

I start peeling the label off the beer bottle. My nail catches the top right corner, lifts the label just enough so I can hold it between my thumb and index finger then slowly pull the paper down, attempting to release the entire label in one peel.

"I've seen Jacob do that," Ken says.

"We used to peel the paper off bottles whenever we drank together. The goal is to free the paper without a tear. The loser has to drink a shot of whiskey."

"Who usually won?"

"About even. Sometimes we lost on purpose." I smile.

"He was always competitive," Ken says. "I can't think of anything I was better at than Jacob. He even got the prettiest girls, though he didn't brag. If someone bested him, you could see the pressure build. Did he ever blow up on you?"

"No. He was just hard on himself."

"Why was Cindy there?" Ken asks.

"She drove me to the funeral."

"Why was she with you at the funeral home?"

"She didn't want me to be alone."

"What was she doing outside my office?"

"Waiting for me," I reply and begin again to peel the label.

"Why not wait in the car?"

"Too dark."

"What were you girls up to?"

"Not girls. We're over sixty."

"You know what I mean."

"No, I don't."

"I think you and Cindy were up to something."

I keep peeling the label.

"What's your theory?" I ask.

"I don't have one. The way she popped through my office door and announced she was ready to go made me wonder if she'd accomplished a mission."

"You talk like we're a couple of spies."

"Cindy appeared to be through with whatever she was doing and was pretty pleased with herself."

"You got us, Ken. We stole a key to the coffin, went to the cemetery, and dug Jacob up so I could see if he shot himself." I offer him an Oreo. He shakes his head.

"Okay. Don't tell me."

"I won't."

"You never answered me. How you holding up?"

"Not great. I'm just a bitch, Ken."

"Aren't we all sometimes?"

"Jacob believed that he failed as a writer and carried an abiding fear of being found out. He couldn't face Trion, and I wanted him to move back. The night he passed, I threatened to cut him off if he didn't return."

Ken leans back in his chair, pats his leg, and Willy jingles over. Ken scratches him behind his ear, and Willy makes a satisfying growl.

"You can't kill somebody by telling them you'll cut them off," he says. "You didn't cause Jacob's heart attack. Maybe he had a weak heart all along and hid it from everybody. Maybe the cause was diet and drinking. God knows he drank like a fish when I saw him every now and then. Maybe he started smoking again like you."

"I bummed a couple from Cindy."

"I'm not accusing you of anything. I'm just trying to talk some sense into you."

Pushing back my chair and startling Willy, who leaves Ken to sit next to me with his eyes on Ken, I say, "I thought you couldn't stay long."

"I bury people," he says. "I also see who's left when people die. I know I'll be burying some of them within the year, those who can't accept that their husband or wife, son or daughter is gone. They feel blame."

"I know about survivor's guilt."

"Not this kind," he says. "Some folks who've given part of themselves to the body in the casket can't go on living without what they've given away. Not that the ones who can go on living loved the dear departed any less. They just kept more for themselves. They gave what they could but couldn't give all they had. My dad loved my mom and remarried fifteen months after she died."

"I divorced Jacob."

"I know. You surprised everybody. And you never remarried. That didn't surprise me at all," he says.

"Do you think I'll wither and die like some doomed damsel?"

Ken retrieves two more beers from the fridge, opens one, and hands the other to me.

"You just said you thought Jacob killed himself because you threatened to cut him off. If you think he loved you that much, how much do you love him? Do you have a gun?"

"He shot himself?"

"He died of a heart attack," Ken says louder than usual.

"I don't believe you, and I don't have a gun."

We drink more of our beer. Ken starts to peel his label and tears it when only a third's released. I smile a smile that wouldn't look good on a corpse. I want to forget. All of it. The love, the hurt, the betrayal — Jacob's and mine. All his stories I've read and edited, all the late-night calls. I want it all gone.

"Fuck me," I say to Ken.

He begins to speak and stops. He doesn't look surprised, so maybe this was the real reason he came over: to comfort the grieving ex-wife. It's a cliché, a scene from an old movie. I don't care tonight. I walk to the bedroom and wait. He follows. I turn off the lights, and neither of us utters a word. We lay on the bed and he kisses my neck. He pulls off his shirt and trousers as I kiss his arms and chest. He fingers me until my thighs are wet, and he pushes inside me so hard I scream, and he pushes harder. Only Jacob has ever given me an orgasm like that, making me feel I've left this earth for another existence. I fall back in oblivion and Ken rolls over.

"Do it again," I say, playing with his nipples.

I stare at the ceiling and think any minute it may collapse. Any minute I may sink into the earth and never return. Then the night comes back. Ken's not Jacob. I want Jacob there.

"I better get back to the funeral home before they call the cops on me," Ken says, putting on his clothes. "Will you be okay?"

"No," I say, "but I'm not going to do anything stupid."

I kiss him again. "Thanks, Ken."

He kisses me on the head and walks toward the door. "You know he was my best buddy."

"I guess that makes it all right," I say.

"I wish Jacob had died of a heart attack," Ken says as he walks into the dark.

*I'm back in court on the witness stand.*

*Susan's Lawyer: We now have evidence that Jacob Hall committed suicide. Does this change your testimony in anyway?*

*Janet: I don't know.*

*Susan's Lawyer: We can never know with a hundred percent certainty, and this court doesn't require a hundred percent certainty. Can you state a probability, if you'll excuse the cliché, that your threat pushed him over the edge?*

*Janet: I think a reasonable doubt exists. What probability would include a reasonable doubt? Sixty? Seventy?*

*Susan's Lawyer: Ms. Hall, this is a civil procedure. We only require a preponderance of the evidence. Your estimate that you are seventy percent sure your threat caused his suicide would constitute a preponderance. Let me rephrase. Is it more likely than not that your threat caused him to kill himself?*

*Janet: I can't answer that.*

*Susan's Lawyer: Why not?*

*Janet: I didn't know he was suicidal. You can't know what anyone else is really thinking or feeling. I'm not omniscient. I knew Jacob better than anyone. He gave no hint of harming himself.*

*Susan's Lawyer: If you are not guilty of causing his suicide, you are guilty of not knowing the man you claim was the love of your life. You read everything he wrote. You knew him better than his sister, better than his children. But you didn't really listen to his despair. You didn't try to comfort him. You told him*

*my way or the highway. Did you enjoy the payback? Was it nice being on top?*
  *Janet (crying): Yes. Yes, it was.*

I stand in the doorway and gaze into the night, listening to my heart. I did kill him. My threat triggered his drunken self who talked of suicide as if it were some intellectual state of being. A place where the individual can exert control over fate, where regrets are meaningless words. I didn't take him to the cliff. Although, blind to where we were, I did push.

My buzz is gone. Whatever pleasure I felt with Ken left with Ken. Sensing my pain, Willy sits by my side. I open the door and follow him, again hoping for a few fireflies

But I was on a country road in North Alabama on a Sunday morning. Not knowing where I stood or how to retrieve my car, I looked back, hoping to see Georgia's Ford F-150. No truck appeared. No tires on the road could be heard. Only the sounds of insects and the beating of my empty heart.

—Jacob Hall, "Behold, I Give You the Power"

# Chapter 27

The Williams House
Sunday, September 15, 2019
9:30 a.m.

Waking with a splitting headache, I lie in bed and wait for the pain to subside so I can open my eyes. The dull ache at the back of my neck reminds me that deep sadness can't be washed away. Toward the end of our marriage, Jacob and I often had mornings like this after a long night of drinking and sex. By then the sex had become more physical, less loving. My body often felt used and vacant, though the orgasms were more frequent and intense.

Ignoring Rhoda, I lie lost in the past until I hear someone pounding on the door. Willy begins to bark, and Rhoda runs off to hide. Easing off the bed, I wrap the bathrobe around me and walk to the front. Grabbing Willy's collar, I open the door, and Susan stands behind a big corrugated box.

My eyes still gummy, I ask, "What time is it?"

"I'm on my way to early church and thought you might want this."

I let go of Willy's collar, and he runs out to the nearest bush before I call him back.

"Want a cup of coffee?"

"Don't mind if I do," she says, sliding the box with her feet over the threshold.

"What is that?"

"Jacob's writing. He left it to you. I wanted to read some first, but after hearing Crystal read part of his story at the funeral yesterday, I decided to get his writing out of the house before she got her hands on it. She's already put him on a pedestal."

"Who doesn't?"

"I'm afraid she might follow in his footsteps and leave Trion. I don't want her to see him—or you, for that matter—as a model."

"Don't worry about me," I say and put on the coffee. "Still take it black?"

She nods as she sits down, and I see the cost of the last week on her. Going to church isn't going to solve the problem but may bring her some relief. I steal a cup from the pot, hand it to her, give Willy some food, and pour myself a cup.

"Thanks." She blows on the coffee, takes a sip, and smiles. "First thing today, Larry brought me a cappuccino in bed. He's been into espresso the last six months and bought some strange Italian machine. Now he's working hard on latte art. This morning it was a rose. I wouldn't have known unless he'd told me. Looked like a white lump. He's trying to figure out what he's going to do when he retires."

"Isn't golf enough?"

"Not really. He mainly plays to be social. He doesn't have much interest in the game. I'm glad. I think most of those guys use it as an excuse to drink."

"I started teaching again, part-time, because I was bored. What are you going to do when Crystal goes to college?"

"Fret and go to a bunch of football games."

"I asked Jacob to come back here when he retired."

Susan's eyes begin to tear. I look away at Willy.

"You said he didn't like Trion."

"I didn't know I could come back either until Aunt Grace left me her house. I think coming back could have been the same for Jacob."

"You got him to leave. You could have gotten him to return. The one thing in this world he loved more than writing was you. Nora and the girls knew that."

"They told me," I say.

"Did you ever reach them last night?"

"Nora told me to leave them alone."

"I'm glad Crystal hasn't spent much time with those two cousins," Susan says and glances at her watch, a small traditional face surrounded by diamonds.

"They're strange," I say.

"You know Jacob did have a heart attack."

"Don't worry," I say.

"Gotta go. Thanks for the coffee."

I watch Susan's SUV pull out of the drive and turn left on the highway. Then I look down at the box. Just like Susan to rummage through something intended for me. Suspecting Pandora's box held less trouble, I drag the container into the kitchen, its bulk almost crowding me to the side. Glaring at its intrusive presence, its bulged middle and worn flaps, I circle around it, a fifteen-year-old girl again, my words trapped in my throat.

Meowing and looking at me with her green kitty-cat eyes, Rhoda appears. In fewer than twenty-four hours, Willy has learned his place under the table, thumping his tail. I fix breakfast and pour another cup of coffee. Pressing my fingers against my eyes, I look into a black abyss with sparkling holes. Here's the essence of Jacob. The writer who spent most of his adult life shaping and forming words, getting them out for himself and the readers he envisioned. If only he'd kept his confidence and believed in himself, instead of relying on external acclaim, he could have continued to live in the world he imagined, full of life and death, grief and grace, the very stuff of existence.

I doubt there's anything here I haven't read. If I hadn't already smoked Crystal's joint, this would be the perfect time to light up and drift into bliss. I take a swallow of black coffee and lean over the box, raising it flaps like the wings of a bird to expose reams of manuscript sheets beneath.

The inside smells of mildew, the odor of a basement after warm, humid air condenses on cool surfaces. When I visited Jacob in Illinois, the first thing I did was open the windows and turn on the fans to disperse the staleness. In his later years, he became oblivious to smell, blaming his sinuses. His way of living was to write and fuck and teach, in that order. He ate frozen Lean Cuisines and canned beans from pinto and butter beans to red beans and black-eyed peas. Fresh air was of no concern.

I pull out a handful of paper and lay the pages on the table. Willy walks around sniffing the box, stopping and starting, until he inspects all sides. Unwilling to leave that familiar scent, he lies between it and me, his fur against my ankle. Sifting through the paper, I see stories I edited long ago, some of which he'd published and continued to revise. He was meticulous, obsessively so, never thinking a piece fully finished.

With each page I feel closer to him.

"Janet, I'm not done. The ending is wrong," he'd say.

"You've been working on this story two years. The editor wants it now. Otherwise, why the phone call?"

"It's not ready."

"It never will be. Give it to me," I'd say, yanking it from his hand and sending it out.

Sorting these pages, I hear that scenario over and over. It never changes. He relied on me, more and more, as editor. He craved solitude to create, never feeling the absence of people since he was so absorbed in the characters he created. They were his company, his connection to the world, and I was their caretaker, the one who assured they'd be clean, well fed, and in proper attire before sent into the world.

"Jacob, I need more in life than your writing."

I hear my past lament with every sheet I touch. These stacks of words, his words, are Jacob all around, Jacob transparent. Though I've read these stories many times, now holding the paper and seeing the type make the words all the more intimate. They are his, they are Jacob. He is here with me as he's always been. I can feel him beside me, over me, on top of me breathing against my skin, his warmth enveloping me. His writing, this box of words, are the clearing, the space between life and death where the body passes into spirit and immortality. These fragments of stories, essays, works in progress are Jacob. He passed them on to me. I'm again the caretaker, a role I know too well. A posthumous collection of his old and new stories, posthumous editions of his two novels. Is this what he intended by leaving me his work? Imposing his sense of falling short of expectations onto me? Am I to feel responsible for picking up the pieces and getting them out into the world? Is this to be my final act of contrition for divorcing him?

I can edit and arrange them for publication. I can ensure that he receives the notice and accolades his writing deserves. Who better to pass along his work, create his legacy? How can I not accept this responsibility for the man who took my hand and led me out of Trion to an astounding world of books and dreams? How can I resist?

I feel my phone vibrate. A text message from Cindy.

```
What ru doing?
Going thru Jacob's papers.
???
Susan brought me a box of his writing this morning.
Why?
He wanted me to have them.
The dog wasn't enough?
He probably treasured his writing more. Later.
```

The sun comes through the kitchen window, shining on half the box. The other half stays a dark shade of beige. I feel the despair of a great sadness. Not so much the loss of Jacob as the loss of something I can't articulate. Cleaning herself, Rhoda is on top of the table at the other end, her back leg raised, front paws anchoring, ignoring Willy and me. He's scratching the back door and whining to go out. I open the door and he flies into the yard, looking back for me. Willy is a gift who'll demand walks and pets and baths, unlike Rhoda, who makes a fuss only when her food dish is empty. I watch Jacob's Labrador dig around the azalea bush then run back to me and jump on my legs then run back to the azalea and dig again, repeating the runs and jumps until I'm tired from just watching.

Labs are lively, highly energetic dogs, and I'm willing to make some concessions for Willy. He's digging next to Aunt Grace's galvanized trash can where she burned leaves in November and Christmas debris in December. The city now provides bins on rollers, making it easier for garbage collection every Friday.

I return to the kitchen and look at the papers covering my table and recall the way they cluttered our life when we first married, sheets hanging from clotheslines attached from wall to wall all over the apartment, scattered across the bed and table and in the corners. Pages covered every possible space, pushing me out, out of the bedroom to the living room, out of the apartment to the library. Out of my own life. One night I dreamed I was buried alive under stacks of paper. Hyperventilating alone in the bed, I woke, the light from the kitchen slipping under the bedroom door.

I start to feel that claustrophobia in his passing. He had enough difficulty sending out his own work. Now he'd left it all to me, some stories published, some half written, others unrevised. The very thing that broke our marriage. When Jacob was living, I could bear the weight of his writing. I can't abide it without him.

The kitchen table now buried under his pages, my eyes focus on his leavings. Covered in the past, I sit down. Damn it, Janet. Are you going to surrender again? Give your life to him? What happened to the Janet who left to find herself? She loved him; however, she didn't love what she'd become with him.

After picking up an armful of papers, I grab a box of wooden matches with blue tips next to the stove and walk outside. I put the pages on the ground under a brick and pull them out, one by one, light a match, and witness the ends curl into black ash with a hint of fiery red. I dangle the first page until it's almost gone, just a fragment with a silver edge between my thumb and index finger before dropping it in the can. Pulling out another sheet, I light it and gaze at the soft burn. For nearly an hour I burn paper. This is his funeral pyre, his writing turned to smoke, circling upward in cumulous clouds. Ashes left in its wake.

I'm adding more sheets to the fire when Miss Irene saunters over to the fence.

"Not sure we're supposed to use our burn barrels anymore," she says.

"Probably not," I agree and add another handful.

"It's not like there's a drought after all," she replies.

"Guess I ought to take them to the new recycling center by Piggly Wiggly, but I doubt I will."

"Fair enough. You made it through yesterday."

"Barely."

"I always took a certain pleasure in tossing out old student work," she says. "You know that you'll get to start all over again the next semester. Phoenix rising from the ashes."

I add more paper. Willy runs over to the fence and looks at her.

"I've meant to ask where the dog came from."

"Jacob. He left Willy to me in his will."

"Odd thing to do," Miss Irene says and heads back toward her house.

When the burning's done, I drag the hose over and kill the embers. Willy jumps at the stream of water. Opening the nozzle, I let him drink from the hose and join him, remembering how we all drank from hoses back in the day. No bottles of French or Canadian spring water. Just a simple need filled by the simplest means. Afterward, Aunt Grace would set up the sprinkler for us to run through. I dig the sprinkler out of the garage, and Willy and I run through it. In the mist rainbows form, only to disappear.

I hear the strange sound of my laughter. Willy stops running and barks. Why is he upset with me? He's not. He's warning of a car in the driveway. Dressed for church in shades of blue, Clara steps out. In her hands is a bright pink box that I hope holds something sweet. Walking toward me, she smiles. I stand there, drenched. Willy runs to greet her, and I shake off the water before following.

# About the Author

With a Ph.D. in British and American literature and an MFA in poetry, Chella Courington is a writer and teacher who's published ten chapbooks of poetry and five of fiction. Her many stories and poems appear in a range of journals and anthologies including *SmokeLong Quarterly, The Collagist,* and *New World Writing.* Her poetry has been nominated for *Best of the Net* and *Best New Poets* along with awarded individual prizes, the most recent of which is *Writing in a Woman's Voice Moon Prize* for her poem "Eurydice." Her fiction also has been nominated for *Best of the Net, Best Small Fictions,* and *Pushcart* as well as awarded individual prizes, the most recent of which is the *Shooter Magazine Flash Prize* for "Showtime."

She lives in Southern California with another writer, two kitties (Simone de Beauvoir and Guy de Maupassant), and two puppies (Marcel Proust and Jean-Paul Sartre).

Follow Chella at:

Twitter: @chellacouringto

Instagram: https://www.instagram.com/chellacourington/

Amazon:https://www.amazon.com/s?i=stripbooks&rh=p_27%3A Chella+Courington

Author Page: https: chellacourington.net

Facebook: https://www.facebook.com/chella.courington/

Facebook Author Page:
https://www.facebook.com/profile.php?id=100063484093419

Facebook Janet Hall by Chella Courington:
https://www.facebook.com/profile.php?id=61564269435957

Goodreads https://www.goodreads.com/user/show/4606922-chella

* 9 7 9 8 9 8 9 4 5 1 3 6 4 *